INTRIGUED

THE DARK BILLIONAIRE

Z.L. ARKADIE

Arrival

HOLLY HENDERSON

DECEMBER 21ST

"I can't believe how lucky I am!" That's what I keep telling myself ever since I accepted Bronwyn Henrietta Blackstone's invitation. She offered me a two-in-one deal—to spend the week before Christmas with her family and take on a project to pay off the debt I owe them. The only catch is, I have no idea what the job entails.

"Is it even legal?" I asked her during our call, feeling a bit annoyed because she seemed to be whispering.

Ever since I first met Bronwyn, it's clear she enjoys being mysterious. Even the way we became roommates at Redmond College remains half-shrouded in secrecy. Redmond, an exclusive all-girls college on the East Coast, is where the wealthy and privileged send their daughters to carry on their blue-blooded family legacies. In stark contrast, I come from humble beginnings. My family's financial struggles were never a secret—I'm the daughter of a conman and a perpetually depressed woman who passed away too soon. But despite all that, school has always been my sanctuary. I have a passion for learning and graduated at the top of my class, which earned me a full academic scholarship to Redmond College.

"Yes, it's legal," Bronwyn whispered, and her response held a hint of offense at my question.

"Okay, then just tell me what you want from me," I insisted, eager for answers.

"I can't. Not over the phone."

"Why not?"

"Holly, please don't make this more difficult than necessary. Trust me, you're going to have a lovely time. Besides, what I need from you aligns perfectly with your expertise."

I frowned, feeling puzzled. "My expertise?"

"Investigative reporting," she revealed.

My eyes widened, and I sat up straight in my chair. "Oh. Okay..."

"I also know that you're an independent reporter. I've read both of your books, 'The Howsley Project' and 'In Defense of Bad Air.'"

"You did?" I asked in astonishment, my voice hitting a higher pitch. I glanced absentmindedly at the large downtown building on the opposite side of the bustling avenue. Bronwyn had done her homework, which wasn't like her unless it served a significant purpose for her.

"Yes, I did," Bronwyn confirmed.

I had sold many copies of my books, but hearing that she, someone from my early days, had read them felt both strange and incredibly gratifying.

"I promise it will be worth your while," she whispered even softer than before, piquing my curiosity even more.

Now, here I am, having accepted her invitation and driven four long hours from Philadelphia to Newport, Rhode Island. I sit in the driver's seat of my modest car, facing the grand entrance of the Blackstone mansion estate. The massive iron gates, adorned with pointy spears and the family crest, slowly open wide, inviting me into their famous and exclusive property.

Nerves flutter in my stomach as I carefully drive

past pine trees adorned with glistening fresh snow and wide, pristine lawns, approaching the rustic red stone mansion. It's a sight to behold, with its high, pointy gables that resemble an old church, and picture windows radiating a warm glow across the brick facade. Several chimneys peak beyond the roof like narrow spires, sending smoke billowing into the opaque white sky. Despite the harrowing rumors surrounding the Blackstone family mansion, from where I sit, it exudes an aura of warmth and life.

Finally, I reach a fork in the drive and decide to curve towards the front of the house. Bryn hadn't given me any specific instructions on where to park or what to do upon my arrival. The rush to finish all my assignments before the holidays made me forget to call and confirm the details. All I have is the address and the family gate code. However, we did agree that I'd be arriving between 3:00 p.m. and 5:00 p.m. I glance at the time on the console—it's 3:17 p.m. I park the car in front of a long walkway and peer past the black iron gates that enclose a quaint patio. The front doors remind me of ancient bronze castle gates, looking like they haven't been opened in centuries.

I let out a heavy sigh as I lean back against the

driver's seat. I should've planned my arrival better. But amidst my worries, a question lingers in my mind—would I even recognize Bronwyn today? It's been so long since we last saw each other. We said goodbye after our first year of college, expecting to room together the next year. But she never showed up. For junior and senior year, I ended up in the same dorm room, but she was nowhere to be found. I tried calling her several times, only reaching one of the family estate secretaries, who promised to relay my messages to her.

During college, I lived in the most luxurious dorm on campus, which I later discovered wasn't a coincidence. Lost in thought, I stare out through my windshield, recalling the first time I met the stunning, wealthy heiress with her perfect blond ringlets and captivating eyes. It was during our welcome orientation in the main sanctuary, two weeks before classes started.

As I sat alone in the large, buzzing auditorium, I couldn't help but feel like an outsider. The room was packed with girls who seemed to all know each other, as if they had spent summers at some glamorous camp in the Alps or a similar luxurious destination. Their conversations revolved around which expensive private high schools they attended, and there were discussions about some girls who didn't make the cut to attend Redmond due to their grades.

Then came the moment that made me feel like a true outsider. Overhearing a conversation nearby, I suddenly realized they referred to some of us as "hobos." I felt a pang of hurt as the girl with dark hair and strikingly large eyes shot a glare in my direction after making that hurtful comment.

It stung to be labeled that way, to be seen as someone who didn't belong. I hadn't come from wealth and privilege like the others, and it seemed that made me an easy target for their judgment.

Still reeling from the earlier hurtful comment, I was taken aback when a bold girl plopped down in the seat beside me. Her words were shocking and unfiltered, but in some strange way, it felt like she was defending me. "Don't mind them. They're stinky little bitches with bad breath and sour pussies," she said, her tone unabashed and assertive.

While I appreciated her standing up for me, her language was quite coarse, and I couldn't help but gasp at her choice of words. Nonetheless, it seemed like her response had wounded the girls who had been mocking me earlier, and I felt a glimmer of relief.

With a newfound sense of camaraderie, she introduced herself, "I'm Bronwyn Blackstone, but the people I like call me Bryn."

One of the girls within the group surreptitiously glanced in our direction, seemingly cautious not to offend. It became evident that using Bryn's nickname was likely a privilege only granted to a select few, further solidifying her position at the top of the rich and powerful pecking order.

She asked for my name and I tentatively said, "Holly, Holly Henderson."

"Where did you grow up, Holly Henderson?"

Eyebrows pulled, I said, "Final destination, Pittsburgh."

That seemed to intrigue her and so she asked, "What does your father do?"

I narrowed an eye baffled by her forwardness. "You mean for work?"

"Yeah..." She waited attentively for my answer.

Thanks to the support of a wonderful principal, guidance counselors, and teachers, I had learned not to let my father's actions define me. "Absolutely nothing," I replied firmly, standing tall.

Bryn's laughter filled the air as she tossed her head back, exclaiming, "I like you." She shifted in her seat, turning her body towards me with an air of intrigue. "You don't know who I am?"

I leaned back, giving her a once-over, and replied honestly, "Should I know who you are?"

Her smirk turned smug as she responded, "Maybe. Maybe not."

Our conversation was cut short when Dean Westerly stepped onto the stage, addressing all the new students at Redmond. Before I could say anything else, Bryn stood up and sauntered out of the auditorium with an air of self-assurance, as if she owned the world. I couldn't help but wonder what role she played in this enigmatic college.

A week later, I walked into what felt like my version of heaven on earth—my new dorm room. It resembled a luxury apartment, complete with all the amenities one could imagine. Two master bedrooms with attached bathrooms, and even a jetted tub that left me in awe. I checked the tag attached to the key my student advisor had given me, confirming that this was indeed my assigned room, despite the opulence that seemed beyond my expectations.

"Hey, roomie," a familiar voice called out.

I turned around to find Bryn standing there, accompanied by a cute guy with floppy hair and a bad boy smirk—I later got to know him as Dale Rumor.

With a cocky smile, she declared, "I needed a roommate, so I chose you."

It didn't take long for me to realize that Bryn had deliberately befriended me during orientation because she was searching for someone like me—an outsider with no connections to her world of secrets. As I soon discovered, the Blackstone family's wealth was beyond comprehension, and Bryn was determined to keep her double life hidden from any gossip and scandal.

Fortunately, my past had taught me to keep to myself and respect others' privacy. Bryn seemed to bring a new guy home almost every night, but I didn't pry or judge. Some of them would stay the night, while others would leave after spending several hours locked in her room. I couldn't help but find it peculiar that they remained so hushed during their visits.

However, Bryn and I had formed a genuine bond over time. She was a great listener and always lent an ear as I poured out my heart about the struggles my parents put me through. In return, she seldom spoke about her own family, although I knew she had a twin brother and two older brothers. Like my parents, her wealthier yet seemingly unstable parents never bothered to visit. Occasionally, a woman would come by to check on Bryn, but she remained tight-lipped about the woman's identity and their relationship.

After graduation, I was taken aback when I received a handwritten card from Bryn. It said, "Don't worry about paying us back for the dorm. You deserve to live in the lap of luxury." I had assumed my scholarship covered my room and board expenses, but it turned out that Blackstone Family Enterprises had been footing the bill. The revelation left me astonished, but I couldn't accept such generosity without repaying them.

As soon as I landed my first job as a reporter, I reached out to the estate and made arrangements to repay them. Over the last three years, I've been paying them eight hundred dollars a month, working diligently to clear my debt. With thirty-six thousand dollars left to go, I'm determined to fulfill my obligation. *But what does she want me to do? I hope it's legal.*

I turn my gaze toward the imposing doors, knowing that I'll soon come face-to-face with Bryn again. I wonder if she's changed much over the years. There are no recent pictures of her online, not that I've actively searched for them. She hasn't occupied my thoughts in a long time. Occasionally, her older brother Jasper comes to my attention, but everyone knows better than to mess with him. Well, almost everyone—there's a colleague of mine who's obsessed with bringing the Blackstones down. Regardless, I remember Bryn as a stunning beauty back in college, and I doubt that has changed.

"Here goes nothing," I mutter with a sigh. I twist my body and reach into the back seat, quickly grabbing my ankle-length wool coat. The thick, warm coat is like a ninja warrior, expertly battling the cold. My hand then searches beneath the passenger seat to retrieve my purse. "Got it," I whisper triumphantly, though my arm aches from the effort of performing just two actions in such a confined space. My compact car might be fuel-efficient, but it certainly isn't the most comfortable vehicle.

My heart races as I press my hand against my chest, leaning closer to the car window to get a better look. A man stands on the other side, and his intense gaze feels like it's piercing right through me. I take a moment to absorb his features—a masterpiece of angles and the most enticing lips I've ever seen. His whole face is just... Wow. It's as if he has the power to hypnotize with a simple glance, like a medallion swaying back and forth.

He takes a step back, and his commanding voice breaks through the momentary trance. "Roll down the window," he orders, motioning for me to comply.

I steady my breaths and press the button on the armrest to open the window.

He folds his arms, exuding an air of authority akin to a highway patrolman handing out a well-deserved speeding ticket. "Who are you, and how did you get through my gate?" he demands.

I slap my hand on my chest lightly, a hint of annoyance in my tone. "I'm Holly Henderson." I expect him to recognize the name as one Bryn mentioned, but his stern expression doesn't falter. "Bryn invited me for the holiday, and..." It finally dawns on me. I'm face to face with one of Bryn's brothers—and I know which one.

The extremely handsome man outside my car door is none other than Jasper Walker Blackstone, the eldest brother and a potential presidential candidate. Holy shit. Is he the reason why I'm here? Does Bryn want me to interview her brother? I have a reputation for exposing powerful and shady figures like him. A favorable interview from me could paint him in an immaculate light, which is why I'm hesitant about taking on such a task.

"You're Bryn's friend?" he questions, his tone accusatory.

"Yes," I respond, trying to keep my composure despite the adrenaline coursing through me. "And you're Jasper Blackstone."

His eyes narrow, and I can sense that he's thinking something, but whatever it is, it doesn't seem welcoming. "She didn't inform me that we were having guests this week," he says coolly.

I press my lips together, tempted to comply with his unspoken desire to turn around and head back home. Part of me wants to say, "Alright, thanks, and see you never." But instead, I remain silent, curious to see how this encounter will unfold. There's something intriguing about Jasper, something that piques my journalist instincts even as I tread cautiously. *But what a prick.*

"Well, you can't park here," he grumbles, his annoyance palpable. His gaze shifts towards the fork in the drive, the very spot where I had stopped earlier. "It's going to snow in a few hours. Turn around, go back to the split in the drive, and make a left at the back of the house. I'll guide you to the garage."

Before I can even thank him for the assistance, he walks away, leaving me slightly taken aback. It seems showing hospitality isn't one of his strong suits. As he passes the iron gates, they open automatically for him, further reinforcing the impression that he carries himself like a man who believes he owns the world. And perhaps he does. Yet, I can't deny that he looks very attractive in his well-fitted casual dress pants and a thick black winter coat. I catch myself wondering how he smells; I'm certain guys like him always have an enticing scent.

"Get a grip, Holls," I whisper to myself, trying to quell the unexplained emotions that are stirring within me. My slightly trembling hands clench the steering wheel as I execute a three-point turn to follow his instructions. What's wrong with me? I've encountered men who are just as handsome and intimidating as Jasper in the past. But there's something about him that affects me differently, an odd effect I can't quite explain.

Driving at a snail's pace, I can't help but admire Jasper's striking figure as he stands by the driveway. I wonder which of Bryn's brothers I'll encounter next—maybe the charismatic playboy, Spencer, or the brainy chemist, Asher. But for now, I'm face to face with the brawn of the family— Jasper, the muscle. And oh my God, just look at him. He's undeniably captivating.

As I approach him, he motions for me to follow, leading me toward a garage with several car stalls. His walk is hypnotizing, and I find myself drawn to him despite any reservations I may have. He's simply mesmerizing.

One of the garage doors opens automatically, revealing a designated parking spot. Carefully, I steer my car into the stall, knowing that soon I'll be standing mere feet away from Jasper.

"Hi. Thank you for having me," I practice my greeting under my breath, even though his demeanor doesn't exactly exude warmth or excitement at my presence.

I ensure my vehicle is perfectly aligned before switching off the engine. My heart pounds in my chest as I gather my coat and purse from the passenger seat, quickly tucking a forgotten fast-food bag out of sight. I let out a frustrated sigh, annoyed at myself for feeling so self-conscious about how Jasper will see me. He's undoubtedly never indulged in a french fry from a paper bag in his entire life. I brace myself as I open the car door, ready to face his intense, captivating gaze that seems to have a hypnotic effect on me.

"Hello, ma'am," a middle-aged gentleman in a black suit greets me with impeccable manners.

"Hi," I respond, feeling a bit flabbergasted by the formal welcome.

"I'm William, your guest butler," he introduces himself, bowing his head slightly in a deferential manner.

I slip on my coat and begin to introduce myself, but he interjects smoothly, "Holly Henderson, I know. Miss Blackstone informed me of your arrival."

I'm taken aback, pleasantly surprised that my arrival had indeed been anticipated. Finally, someone at the Blackstone estate seems to be aware of my presence, and it makes me feel more at ease. I nod gratefully, thankful that Bryn had made the effort to let the staff know about my visit.

I walk towards the trunk of my car, intending to retrieve my belongings, but William intervenes with a surprising offer. "Miss Henderson, please do not worry about the luggage. Our staff will bring your things to your room and unpack for you."

My eyebrows shoot up, and I instinctively gnaw

on my lower lip. The idea of strangers rummaging through my personal items makes me slightly uneasy.

"We promise the utmost discretion," William reassures me, seemingly able to read my hesitation.

I wrestle with the urge to decline the offer. But it seems like William has already given instructions, and it's too late to change my mind. Before I know it, two young women dressed in blue maid uniforms are making their way toward us.

Feeling slightly awkward, I agree to their help, trusting in William's assurance of discretion. With mixed feelings, I watch as they whisk away my belongings.

Then, an unexpected issue arises with the garage door repeatedly going up and down. William apologizes for the inconvenience and attempts to fix the mechanical glitch. Because it's so chilly, and he's consumed by repairing the door, I assure him that I can find my way to my room on my own, not wanting to impose any further. Reluctantly, he provides me with directions.

Without wasting any time, I swiftly make my way up the drive, eager to explore the Blackstone ancestral home without a chaperone. The sprawling mansion looms ahead, its majestic presence evoking a mix of awe and curiosity within me. I take in every detail—the towering pillars, the ornate architecture, and the air of mystery that surrounds the estate.

As I step inside through the back door, I find myself in a vast, open space adorned with pristine white marble floors. The ambiance is accompanied by gentle instrumental music playing softly in the background, reminiscent of elevator tunes. I can't help but feel a mix of elegance and formality as I take in my surroundings.

Before me stands the curving stairwell that William had mentioned, leading to the upper levels of the mansion. As I prepare to ascend, a strange sensation tingles on the right side of my face, as if someone's gaze is fixed upon me. I quickly turn in that direction, only to find no one there. It must be my imagination playing tricks on me, or perhaps the aura of the mansion is playing with my senses.

Yet, I can't shake the desire to see Jasper Blackstone again. Despite his aloof demeanor, there's an undeniable pull that draws me to him. I find myself hoping that our next encounter will be more agreeable, that we might find common ground amidst the enigmatic world of the Blackstone family.

Or maybe not.

Why do I even care?

Oh right, he's powerful—very powerful. It'll be great to learn what makes a man like him tick.

Carefully following William's instructions, I ascend the stairway and find myself at the end of the hallway. Two doors, side by side, catch my attention, and I wonder if they lead to the same room. Considering that William emphasized "the right" a few times, I opt to open the door on the right.

As I step inside, my eyes widen in amazement at the grandeur before me. The room is like something out of a royal palace, with a tall king-sized bed adorned in opulent gold silk and a regal, golden-tufted backboard. It's the kind of bed fit for a queen, perhaps even the Queen of England herself. Rich red velvet curtains and beautifully draped valances separate the sleeping area from a luxurious sitting space. An exquisite crystal-encrusted chande-lier hangs gracefully over the bed, adding to the room's grandeur.

My gaze then falls upon the wall of windows, revealing a picturesque view of the snow-covered lawn and the thistle-adorned branches of tall trees. The golden brocade drapes and valances add an extra touch of elegance to the scene.

I can't help but feel a sense of awe and wonderment at the room's lavish decor, so different from my own modern sensibilities. As I glance at my reflection in the gold-leaf framed standing mirror, I realize how out of place I seem with my dark, messy hair and heavy black coat amidst the historical opulence.

Suddenly, I gasp and freeze as I notice him. There he is, Jasper Blackstone, seated in one of the high-backed chairs next to the window. His intense gaze meets mine, and for a moment, time seems to stand still. I feel a rush of nerves and excitement, unsure of how to react to this unexpected encounter.

"I didn't see you," I manage to stammer, my hand pressed against my rapidly beating heart.

"What are you doing in here?" he demands, his tone sharp and commanding.

My mouth falls open, caught off guard by his intense frown and imposing demeanor. His presence fills the room with an aura of power, leaving me momentarily speechless. My mind races to find the right words, but they seem to escape me in his formidable presence.

It's Getting Kind of Strange

HOLLY HENDERSON

My face flushes with embarrassment as I stumble over my words, trying to explain how William directed me to this particular room. However, even to my own ears, my voice carries a hint of doubt. It becomes evident that I must have chosen the wrong door.

"This is not a guest room," Jasper says in a voice so icy, it could freeze lava.

His words sting like a sharp rebuke, and I feel a wave of self-consciousness wash over me.

"Oh," I reply, still unsure why he's scrutinizing me as though I'm a portrait on the wall requiring some level of examination.

"You're an investigative reporter, aren't you?" he finally asks.

"Yes, I am," I respond, my nerves getting the better of me. Perhaps that's the reason for his peculiar gaze—assessing how much of a threat I pose to him and his family.

"How long will you be staying?" he inquires.

I swallow nervously, though I must maintain my composure. "Until the twenty-sixth."

His next words come with a clear warning. "We value our privacy here."

The weight of his statement sinks in, and I realize that I've entered a domain where secrets are guarded closely. Jasper's family has a reputation to protect, and my presence as an investigative reporter might be seen as an intrusion.

I flash him a reassuring smile, hoping to ease the tension, but it only seems to intensify his frown. "Just keep your crimes in the closet, and we'll be peachy keen," I quip, trying to add some lightness to the situation.

However, Jasper's stern expression remains unchanged, and it's evident that he doesn't find my attempt at humor amusing at all. Realizing my misstep, I decide to take a different approach to salvage this awkward encounter.

Walking over to him, I extend my arm for a proper handshake, hoping to convey sincerity.

"Sorry, that was a joke. I can't help myself some-times," I admit, trying to defuse the tension and show that I mean no harm.

He glares at my extended hand as if it has something unpleasant on it, and my stomach churns with worry. I fear I may have made an enemy of the wrong man.

"Sorry," I whisper, my face burning with embar-rassment at my failed attempt to lighten the mood.

Just as I'm about to withdraw my hand, to my surprise, Jasper's large, strong, and surprisingly soft hand gently takes mine. A rush of unexpected sensations courses through me, causing my heart to race. It catches me off guard.

For a brief moment, it feels as though my feet are floating off the floor. Our connection is both intense and fleeting, as Jasper quickly lets go of my hand, allowing his arm to fall back to his side. I'm left wondering if he sensed the tingling energy that passed between us or if it was all in my imagination.

We find ourselves standing in an awkward silence, our eyes locked onto each other. My mind races, searching for something to say or do to break the tension. Goodness, he's incredibly handsome—more captivating in person than any photograph could capture.

"Is this your bedroom?" I manage to ask, my voice strained.

"No," he replies gruffly.

Feeling self-conscious, I cross my arms over my chest, trying to ease my unease. "It's quite stunning," I remark, attempting to find common ground.

Just as I turn to take in the elegant room once more, William's voice interrupts from behind. "Miss Henderson," he calls, standing in the doorway.

I quickly pivot to face him. "A room has been prepared for you next door. I apologize for not being clearer with my directives."

Before I can respond, Jasper interjects, his tone assertive, "She'll stay in this room."

I quickly glance at the attractive Blackstone son, Jasper, and then back at William. I suspect that not showing emotion is a skill William has mastered over the years, yet I catch the subtle wrinkling of his eyebrows and the hint of bewilderment in his eyes. *I wonder why he seems so surprised by Jasper's decision?*

But he doesn't question Jasper's choice. Instead, William calmly says, "I'll have your luggage moved to your new quarters," and then bows before stepping out of the doorway.

As soon as I regain focus on Jasper, he swiftly

passes by me, declaring, "I'll be keeping an eye on you, Miss Henderson."

His intense energy almost sweeps me off my feet, but I manage to whirl around and assert myself. "It's Holly," I respond firmly, offering a more informal address. However, he doesn't acknowledge my request, simply glaring over his shoulder before exiting the room.

Staring at the empty space he left behind, I purse my lips, wondering what in the world I've gotten myself into. Jasper Blackstone is an enigma, and I can already feel the gravity of his presence, pulling me deeper into a web of mystery and intrigue.

———

As the two women enter my new guest room with my luggage, I can't help but feel curious about Jasper and his family. I politely inquire if they mind me assisting with putting away my things. I want to handle it myself, but I also know that the house staff often holds valuable insights into the lives of the residents. They kindly agree, and we begin the task of organizing my belongings.

"So," I inquire, turning my attention to the most

cheerful of the house staff, "what makes this bedroom so special?"

Her grin widens, but there's a hint of hesitation in her response. "All the rooms in the Blackstone mansion are special, Miss Henderson."

I smile and correct her gently, "Actually, please call me Holly."

Her smile is unwaveringly warm. "Miss Henderson, I truly appreciate your modesty and kindness. However, as part of my job, I must ensure you feel at home in the Blackstone mansion. So, with all due respect, I'll refer to you as Miss Henderson."

I smile, understanding that she's just doing her job and respecting the formalities of the mansion. "Alright then, I appreciate your dedication, but you can call me Holly in private. We're going to be spending a lot of time together, and I'd prefer a more relaxed atmosphere when it's just us," I suggest with a warm tone.

She considers my request for a moment before finally nodding in agreement. "Very well, Miss Holly. I will do my best to make you feel comfortable during your stay."

"Thank you," I reply, relieved that we've reached a compromise.

She nods with a hint of relief and leads me into the lavish ensuite bathroom that feels fit for royalty. Together, we carefully arrange my personal items and toiletries on the marble counters and inside the spacious drawers.

Once her co-worker steps out of the bedroom, the maid steps closer until our noses nearly touch, capturing my full attention. Then, she whispers in my ear, "My name is Crystal Preacher. I'm new here, but my mother, Sally Preacher, worked as Amelia Blackstone's personal maid for many years. They were close." Stepping back, she raises her voice and asks, "Will you be needing any more assistance, Miss Holly?"

I'm intrigued, wondering why she shared this information with me. It's as if she knows who I am and wants to establish a connection. "I'm fine, thank you," I reply.

We share a knowing smile, as though we both hold a secret shared only between the two of us, before she gracefully exits the room.

What's the Deal?

HOLLY HENDERSON

Finally, alone, I walk over and flop down in the chair abandoned by Jasper. The cushions smell like cologne, his cologne, so I take a deeper whiff of it. Holy cow, what just happened?

"My goodness, it's true," a familiar voice says. The tone has matured some, but it's still youthful.

I quickly rise to my feet as Bryn seems to float in my direction with her arms open wide.

"You're finally here," I sing, so relieved to see her as we hug.

Bryn leans back to get a full picture of me. "You look well, and beautiful as always."

I allow my gaze to roam her face. She appears

slightly wired but still as beautiful as ever. "Likewise."

We sit, and immediately Bryn squeezes the arms of the chair as she looks around the space as if she's seeing it for the first time. "Jasper put you in this room, huh?"

There's something in her tone that gives me pause. "Yes," I say with a certain amount of ambivalence.

"It belonged to Amelia," she reveals.

My eyes widen. "This is your deceased mother's bedroom?"

"Yes," she says softly and then smiles tightly. "But it's fine."

I take note of the heavy drapes, ornate light fixtures, and bed. No wonder this room feels so antiquated. It's a museum to the late and mysterious Amelia Blackstone. I scratch the side of my neck, suddenly creeped out by the thought of sleeping in the same quarters where a dead woman's memories live.

"How about I move next door to the regular guest room? Really, I don't mind," I say.

Bryn sighs as if she's already bored with this part of our conversation. "Too late. That bedroom is going to be occupied by another guest. Asher's girlfriend, or friend…" She rolls her eyes and shakes her head. "I don't know what they are anymore."

I raise an eyebrow. "Sounds complicated."

Bryn shrugs. "You have no idea."

I feel a twinge of disappointment that the untarnished room has been given away so quickly. But the chill of sleeping in Amelia Blackstone's bed passes, and I turn my attention back to my old friend, Bryn. "So, Bryn, truly, how are you?" I ask, leaning in to catch her response.

Bryn's easy smile is genuine as she answers in her customary whispery voice, "I've been well."

I lean even closer, eager to hear her explanation. "Okay, so, why did you invite me here?" I find myself whispering too, as if drawn into a secret world.

"In due time," she says cryptically, causing my curiosity to pique.

I raise an eyebrow, intrigued by her response. "In 'due time'? What do you mean?"

Bryn smirks playfully. "You'll find out soon enough. Just be ready for dinner at six."

I raise an eyebrow at Bryn's sudden shift in conversation, feeling a bit uneasy. Is she trying to divert my attention from something? I glance around the room, almost expecting to find hidden cameras or listening devices. Knowing Jasper Black-stone's reputation, it wouldn't surprise me if he had the entire mansion wired for surveillance.

"And Holls, I want you to enjoy yourself this week. You are free to use all the facilities on the property—the gym, the pool, the library, etcetera. Oh, and there's a party in two days, you know, for Christmas. You're invited of course."

Despite my suspicions, I manage to smile and nod, playing it cool. "Thanks, Bryn. I'll definitely make the most of my stay here and explore the facilities. And I wouldn't miss the Christmas party for the world."

Bryn asks how my drive was and I go on a rant about all the road closures and rerouting of traffic along the way due to the snow.

"You must be exhausted," she says.

I stifle a yawn, not wanting to give away that I am tired and need some alone time. Bryn and I have always had a special connection. Even when we were roommates, we could sit together in silence and feel completely at ease in each other's presence.

"I'm fine," I say, smiling at her.

Bryn's face lights up as if she's genuinely delighted to see me happy. Then, her hand flies to her throat, and she sighs. "And you were greeted by

Jasper on arrival... I'm so sorry about that. I was..."
She trails off, looking distant for a moment before
returning her gaze to me, sporting a giddy smile.

It's evident that Bryn won't reveal why she
didn't come to greet me. She's still the same secretive Bryn, keeping her secrets close. Right now, I'm
not wearing my reporter's cap, so I won't press her
for answers.

"So, your brother, Jasper…" I say, figuring he's
a much more interesting topic of discussion.

Bryn rolls her eyes slightly. "I'm sorry if Jasper
left a bad taste in your mouth. His bedside manner
needs work. I have no idea how he's ever going to
win an election."

"Yes, there is talk about him running for President," I say. My raised eyebrows and tone
encourage her to tell me more about that.

"Right," Bryn mutters, turning to gaze out the
window. She quickly faces me again and pats my
knee. "But tell me, Holls, are you still single? Or do
you have a boyfriend, fiancé?"

Once again, I'm jarred by the abrupt change in
subject, but I go along with it. "Yes. No. No," I
reply, trying to maintain a pleasant tone.

She crosses her long legs, settling herself into a
more comfortable position as she bursts into a

delighted laugh. "You were always so picky. And to the disappointment of all the boys at Edward Knight Academy."

I take a moment to reminisce about my past self. Back then, I was uptight, serious, and rather plain. There weren't very many boys interested in me, and certainly not the cute and popular ones.

"I would have to disagree with you," I say, giving her knee a light pat. "But never mind me, what about you? Who's filling your love tank these days?"

Bryn groans drearily as her gaze roams the room. "No one's filling love tanks around here."

A chill washes over me, and I can feel it—the darkness that has been lingering in the air all this time. But I choose to ignore that sensation; I must.

"Okay. What about work?" I ask, relieved to shift away from the dead-end conversation about our nonexistent love lives. "What are you doing these days?"

Bryn snorts, her laughter tinged with cynicism. "Have you ever known me to work, Holly?"

I chuckle in response. "No. But I figured eight years after college, you'd find something to do with yourself."

She cracks a tiny smile. "Oh, Holly, how I've missed you."

Raising an eyebrow curiously, I playfully grin. "Then you haven't found something to do with yourself yet?"

A veil of seriousness falls over her face. "That's why you're here."

I narrow my eyes, curiosity piqued. "Why am I here?"

Once again, her gaze rolls around the room before settling on me. "Do you believe in ghosts?" she whispers.

I turn my head slightly to the right, taken aback by the unexpected question. "No, not really. I believe the brain is a very powerful organ. It could make us conjure ghosts, make us see figments of our own making which haunt us."

I wait for her to contradict my statement, as most people do, but she just continues to stare at me.

Feeling a bit uneasy, I shift uncomfortably in my seat. "What?" I inquire.

"I see you're still a pragmatist," Bryn remarks.

Leaning toward her, I keep my voice low. "So you don't want to tell me why you asked me to spend this week with your family because you think a ghost will hear you?"

She leans away from me, and this time her words are clearer, without a whisper. "I invited you to our home because I didn't want you to spend the holidays alone." *What's up with her?*

Frustration builds within me, and I feel the urge to scream. Now I remember how exasperating it can be to have a normal conversation with Bryn Blackstone. There are always several layers of meaning occurring at once, and at any moment, I could abruptly find myself on a new level. I mean, we've only just started talking, and I already feel more exhausted than before we sat down.

I want to call her out, but instead, I manage to say, "Is that so?"

Her jaw sets with determination. "It is so."

I fold my arms over my chest in defiance. "Well, I'm here to work, that's for sure. You said it yourself. Whatever you have in mind for me will absolve me of the debt I owe to your family."

She daintily folds her hands on her lap with carefully crafted composure. "Frankly, Holls, it was you who turned my family's generosity into a debt. You could leave right now if you like, and you still wouldn't have to pay us a dime, and," her lips pull into a small smile, "I will always be your friend. I don't have many of them, but I always felt as though you were one of the few."

I gently fan my fingers over my collarbone, feeling a warm sensation in my heart. I truly believe her. "I'll always consider you a friend as well," I reply, sincere in my words. And she's right, I did turn her family's generosity into a debt. My dad didn't teach me much good, but he did instill in me the belief to never owe anyone a debt because nobody's generous enough to not come collecting. Sooner or later, that debt will come due.

"Okay, well," Bryn sighs as she settles more comfortably in her chair. "I want to tell you more about my experience with Amelia."

I nod eagerly. "I'm listening."

"Unlike you, I believe in ghosts," she says, pointing towards the bed where I'll be sleeping. "I was right over there when Amelia took her last breath, sitting at her bedside. And when I asked her if she was ever going to apologize for being a horrible mother, she said, 'I have nothing to apologize for,' and then looked away."

What a gripping memory. The feeling of what that moment must've been like for Bryn courses through me. "And you didn't press her to explain what she meant?" I ask, curious to know more.

She shakes her head.

Intrigued, I tilt my head curiously. "Do you have any theories?"

Bryn raises a hand, signaling me to stop pushing. Her eyes glisten with tears, but she's determined not to let them fall. Crying has never been her way. I respect that and avert my gaze, giving her a moment to collect herself.

"Then that's it?" I whisper, raising my eyebrows expectantly.

Bryn nods solemnly.

"And you want me to figure out what she meant by that?" I ask, trying to grasp the weight of the situation.

"Yes," she replies, her voice tight with emotion.

"Okay," I mouth, determined to help her find answers. I lean towards her again and whisper, "But what about your brother Jasper?" Just saying his name makes my heart flutter. I wish I knew why he has such an effect on me.

Bryn frowns. "What about him?"

"He warned me to stay out of your family's affairs," I reveal, feeling a hint of concern in my voice.

She twists her mouth, showcasing enough anxiety to make me feel worried.

"Am I going to end up at the bottom of the ocean or something?" I ask, half-jokingly, trying to gauge the seriousness of the situation.

The fact that my question doesn't make her flinch is a tell-tale sign that rumors about Jasper are true—he's dangerous. Instead, she heaves a deep sigh. "I'm not going to downplay Jasper's bark; it does have a bite. But he is very cautious about who he sinks his molars into."

I stretch my mouth squeamishly. "Yikes. That sounds like it hurts."

"He crushes bears. But I will say that he will never hurt me. I'm your safety net," Bryn reassures me.

I grunt thoughtfully, unable to get the image of Jasper crushing bears with his molars out of my head. But instead of feeling repelled by that imagery, I feel something else, a mix of curiosity and a strange attraction.

"What's Jasper's story anyway?"

Bryn frowns confused. "His story?"

"Is he married? Does he have a girlfriend?" I hate that I sound too invested in the answer to my question. I'm sure my interest in her brother is written all over my face.

Her eyes twitch like she's calculating an answer to my question in her head. "I've never seen him with a woman."

"Never?" I sound more surprised than I like.

"No, never."

I sit up straight, feeling my hopes thwarted. "Is he gay?"

"I don't know. It wouldn't surprise me if he were." She points toward the ceiling. "Our dad is upstairs in his sickbed. Jasper probably won't come out of the closet until the axis of evil is dead, buried, and tucked safely away in hell."

My mouth falls open. "Randolph Blackstone is here? And in his sickbed? I hadn't heard any reports of Randolph Blackstone being sick."

"You're not supposed to know that," Bryn says in a voice that lands very much like a warning.

"Understood." I readjust in my seat to reset the tone. "So there's still no love lost between you and your father?"

Her eyes turn colder than when she condemned her father to hell. "Not an ounce."

I clear my throat, trying not to let the hate emanating from her affect my questioning. This conversation has forced me to put on my reporter's cap, and there's no way I'm taking it off. "I take it your father's health isn't getting any better?"

"No." She sounds sure of herself. Suddenly, Bryn rises to her feet. "Why don't you take a bath or shower or whatever you do to decompress before dinner?"

I slowly stand to join her. "Okay."

"And as far as figuring out what the hell Amelia could've meant, I would like for you to do what you do best, Holls," she says.

I frown curiously. "And what's that?"

"Read the table, especially Spencer and Jasper because I believe they know something about our mother they're not telling me. So I'll start the conversation and you tell me what you see?"

Full Disclosure

HOLLY HENDERSON

There was no way I wasn't going to take advantage of the large, deep bathtub. I lay in the warm water, surrounded by bubbles made from sweet vanilla cream liquid soap. Eyes closed, I think about the weird conversation between me and Bryn. I'm certain she screwed up when she revealed that her father was upstairs hanging on for dear life.

Is his room right above this one?

"I have nothing to apologize for," Amelia had said.

I wonder why Bryn just doesn't take her mother at her word. Maybe Amelia wasn't apologetic about being a bad mother. Sometimes parents just don't understand that they're shitty, nor do they care.

I suddenly recall a conversation I'd had with a colleague named Kylie Neeland a while ago about Amelia Blackstone's death, which occurred roughly five years ago.

We had been in a bar at an airport—how cliché, a bar at an airport—just two reporters chatting it up during a layover. Kylie had been determined to make her career off the Blackstones' demise. She knew Bryn was my roommate for one year in college and wondered if I knew how old Bryn's mother was. Apparently, no one could obtain the accurate age of Amelia Rainier Blackstone.

"Isn't that strange?" she asked me.

I couldn't deny that it was. Randolph Blackstone was older than the average father. He'd been seventy when Amelia gave birth to Bryn and he was now ninety-seven. I used to sense Bryn's impatience with her father, as if all she wanted was for him to hurry up and die.

However, Kylie told me this crazy thing she had done following Amelia's death. She'd gotten in touch with the coroner in charge of Mrs. Blackstone's body and had convinced him to give her a tissue sample. However, her plan hadn't worked out. The coroner had gotten arrested for selling body parts and healthy organs on the black market on the morning he was supposed to extract the sample. Just a few hours after that, Amelia Rainier Blackstone's body had been cremated. Kylie and I agreed it was more than a coincidence that the two had happened on the same day.

After heeding Bryn's warning about her brother's bite, I'm now convinced Jasper may have had something to do with the cremation and had covered his tracks so well that Kylie couldn't implicate him.

I open my eyes. The warm water is making me sweat. Or perhaps it's the stress of being attracted to a dangerous and mysterious Blackstone man. I have to get ahold of myself, keep my head in the game, and more importantly, maintain a safe distance from Jasper's sharp molars.

I end my bath, dry off, and massage creamy lotion all over my body. Then I dig deep into the part of my purse where lost items reside and locate the pheromone perfume my former boss Rachel Givens had given me as a parting gift when I decided to become an independent reporter.

She handed me the wrapped box and said, "One day, you will care about attracting a man. When that happens, wear this."

When I'd gotten home and opened her gift, I

found the perfume. I kept it in my purse because I never had many friends, but Rachel was one of them. Keeping her gift with me reminded me that I knew someone who cared about me. But never in a million years could I imagine what I considered a gag gift would come in handy.

I dot the cool liquid on my right then left collarbone. The scent is even driving me wild. For some reason, I feel beautiful as I saunter naked around the room. I brought plenty of nice clothes to wear for dinners and days spent at the Blackstones'. Ultra-wealthy people like this family always have lavish dinners.

I put on my black cashmere dress with a deep V-neck. The material slides across my curves like a gentle kiss on my skin. As I look at myself in the standing mirror, I wonder if I'm over doing it.

There are knocks at the door and I jump startled.

"Yes," I call, sounding composed.

"It's I, Ms. Henderson. William, your butler."

I release the tension in my body. "Please, come in."

The door opens, and William stands in the doorway, his tall frame taking up a lot of space. "Dinner will be served in ten minutes. Please step out when you're ready, and I will escort you to the den for predinner drinks."

Suddenly, I'm so nervous that my breaths become uneven. The time is near. Not only will I see Jasper Blackstone again, but I will be dining with one of the wealthiest and most powerful families in the country. But then I take a slow and deep breath while reminding myself that I have done this before. I have eaten at the White House for goodness' sake. I've attended the Correspondents' Dinner multiple times. *I can do this.*

"I'm ready now," I say.

WALKING THROUGH THE BLACKSTONE MANSION feels like shuffling down the corridors of Independence Hall or any other building that holds its charm from another century. We pass the obligatory portraits of dead men on the wall. People like the Blackstones love showing off their ancestors. After all, without the first entrepreneurs from the Gilded Age, they wouldn't be so wealthy. If I remember correctly, the Blackstones made their fortune from steam trains and railroads first, oil, aircraft service second, then finally technology and investing aggressively in hedge funds and commercial real estate. They are loaded and will be for the rest of their lives.

I follow William down another flight of curved steps then another cold hallway until I see an opened door. Soft orange light spills into the corridor from the room. I expect to hear the chatter of voices. After all, it's cocktail hour and I have two brothers and one possible girlfriend yet to meet. William stops in front of the doorway and points his hand, ushering me inside the room. I say thank you, enter cautiously and then stop in my tracks.

"Jasper?" I whisper, shocked and enthralled by his presence.

His tall and well-built figure stands alone in front of a large window. He reminds me of a portrait that evokes melancholy. It suddenly occurs to me that sadness is the general vibe that Jasper emits. And it's his gloominess that makes me check over my shoulder, looking for the way out. However, part of me wants to escape this scene he has clearly orchestrated and part of me is excited to exist in this moment with him. Then, he turns and I'm trapped in his intense and mesmerizing gaze.

First, Jasper takes me in and I feel restless under

the force of his scrutiny. "Miss Henderson," he whispers.

I swallow nervously and then raise my hands. "What's this all about?"

"Please have a seat," he says, looking at me as though he's distracted by imperfections blotting my face.

Feeling my skin warm, I touch my cheek. "I prefer to stand.

What is that look in his eyes? I'm wondering if he's offended that I didn't sit. He is watching me as though he's able to see my brain processing my thoughts, as if he knows that I'm thinking that looking at him is like admiring a towering hunk of manhood.

Finally, Jasper coughs into his fist to clear his throat. "Let's try this again. Why are you here, Miss Henderson?"

I'm staring into his eyes. They're ferocious but not in an inhuman sort of way. However, I understand that he does mean business. When a man like Jasper Blackstone asks a direct question, he prefers a direct answer. But I'm not one to be bullied by him or anyone else. As far as I'm concerned, I'm an invited guest and that's all he needs to know.

So I set my jaw defiantly. "Bryn knew I'd be

spending Christmas alone, so she invited me to spend the holiday with her family."

Gosh, he's so sexy when he narrows one eye in that way. Actually his face is mere perfection, every part of it.

"I didn't know you were in touch with my sister," he says.

"I wasn't." I figure that's something I don't have to lie about. The jury is still out about whether that was a smart choice or not.

He grunts thoughtfully as if he understands I told the truth and is mildly pleased by it. "And did she get in contact with you or did you contact her?"

I fold my arms. "May I ask why I'm being interrogated by you?"

His eyes narrow, widen, and taper again. Then, he abruptly walks to the bar. "What do you like to drink, Miss Henderson?"

"It's Holly and I'll have tonic water with lemon."

He pauses, holding a bottle of liquor. His eyebrows flash up curiously. "And is that because you need to keep a sober mind?"

I roll my eyes. I mean, this guy is relentless. "Jasper, I'm not here to investigate your family." I turn my head slightly. "Unless there's something you're hiding." *Like your father, who's sick and bedridden.*

All of a sudden, he looks as if he's chewing on an Alka-Seltzer tablet.

I crack a smile. "Just kidding. Goodness, do you ever lighten up?"

He doesn't move a muscle. "Lighten up?"

Suddenly, I feel the expanse of this cozy room, and he and I alone. I think, *what if I continued down this path of openly flirting with him.* Because that's exactly what I just did. By the way he's looking at me, I'm not sure it worked at all.

"Yes," I say hesitantly. "Lighten up."

After a beat he asks, "Red wine?"

I frown confused. "Red wine?"

"We don't have tonic water. Will red wine do?"

There's something in his tone that makes me think something deeper is happening between us at the moment. I'm trying to put the pieces together as I clear my throat, and then croak, "Sure."

Jasper nods sharply, rips his eyes off my face and pours two glasses of red wine. "So, Miss Henderson…"

"Please call me Holly," I nearly beg.

Once again, he studies me curiously. "Don't you like your surname?"

Is he screwing with me?

Okay. I'll play along.

"Not really," I say, walking down whatever road he's setting my feet upon.

Jasper's glower makes my heart skip a beat. My guess is that he's a thinker, the sexy, brooding kind of man with rivers of angst raging deep inside him. And I also think he expected me to wince from the mention of my surname since it's connected to my family pathologies, which I'm certain he knows all about.

"I only call my friends by their first names, Miss Henderson," he whispers while still watching me as if I'm a rare thing.

But his words land hard inside me for some reason—like the jolt of a 7.0 magnitude earth-quake. *Why is he being so goddamn mean?* I get that I'm the enemy, being that I could destroy his family with the power of my pen. But as far as I'm aware, I'm not here for that. *So seriously, dude, chill out.*

And I'm still stewing in an ambrosia of emotions when he whispers, "Your skin looks so soft." Those words slip past his lips like a secret that wasn't supposed to be uttered.

"What did you say?" I ask in a strained voice, even though I heard him clearly.

This period of staring is extremely intense. My head feels floaty and my breaths are ragged. I feel like I might fly and die until Jasper puts his fist over his mouth and coughs, which efficiently makes me drop my eyes to gaze unfocused at the yellow travertine marble floor.

"I have something for you to sign."

I look up to see Jasper walking behind the bar where he produces what is clearly a nondisclosure agreement.

"No," I say bluntly. "I'm not signing that." I have probably never been so offended in my life. "I am your sister's houseguest. If you want me to sign a nondisclosure agreement, then you better have her ask me to do it, not you." I storm right past him, but he takes my arm and I stop in my tracks. One touch and I'm like putty in his hands and he uses my full compliance to guide me against him. The fronts of our bodies press. I can't believe what I'm feeling, on the inside and outside. Jasper Blackstone is as hard as steel, his chest and his cock.

"Why the hell did you come here?" he grumbles, breathing heavily.

My mouth is caught open and I'm lost for words. Jasper releases me as if he's rediscovered his common sense again. But I have been paralyzed by whatever this is I'm feeling. I can't quite name it yet. I don't want to name it.

Then, without another word, Jasper snatches the NDA off the bar top and storms out of the room. What just happened between us seems so surreal.

I take a deep breath and press my hand against my stomach as I steady myself. I would rather return to my room and try to make clear sense out of what just happened between me and Jasper, but I can't. *Holy shit, he had a massive erection. Was it because of me?*

I've just lost composure again, thinking about the possibility of falling in bed with the likes of Jasper Blackstone, so I take another steadying breath.

No way. There's no way at all. Jasper can't want me that way. He's made it very clear that he doesn't want me here at all. So, no. No. No. No. There's no way.

Dinner and Secrets

HOLLY HENDERSON

When I arrive at the dining room, I find four people seated at the long table. I sit next to Bryn. I recognize Bryn's twin brother Asher, sitting next to the woman who must be his girlfriend, Gina. Her neck-length platinum blond hair glistens under the lights of the crystal encrusted chandeliers, three in all, which hang above the table—and her lipstick is bright red. It is by no mistake that her whole style resembles that of Marilyn Monroe. From what I'm able to see, her red cocktail dress is tight and her enhanced breasts are on display thanks to her plunging neckline.

The other brother, who I identify as Spencer, sits slouched in his chair, as if the dinner table is the last place he wants to be. I get the feeling that the family rarely sits down to share a meal together. But, I try to avoid looking at Spencer, who's watching me keenly. He's also gorgeous, and so is Asher. The supremely good-looking gene has definitely been inflicted upon the Blackstone family. The men are tall, all well over six feet. Even Bryn is tall for a woman. She's at least two inches taller than I am, and I'm 5'8".

Surprisingly, the eldest brother has not yet made it to the table, even though a place is set for him. After what happened between us earlier, the anticipation of his arrival makes me antsy.

Spencer scowls at his watch impatiently and then shouts, "Serve the damn dinner!"

A man in uniform nods and walks through a door, which I presume leads to the kitchen. Shortly after, four men wearing similar suits and carrying platters of food enter the dining room and serve our dinner.

I'm so nervous, mostly about social decorum. The food smells delicious. My eyes follow each plate as it's placed carefully on the table.

"So you're Holly Henderson?" Spencer asks.

I snap my attention to him. His smirk is almost

a snarl, and there's definitely nothing welcoming in his eyes.

I sit up straight. "Um, yes."

"I'm not a fan of your books."

My eyebrows flash up in shock. *He dislikes me too?*

"Spencer, she's our guest. Be nice," Bryn scolds.

But I hold my hand up, signaling to her that I can handle this. Frankly, I've had my fill of being pushed around by the Blackstone brothers. "I only write the truth," I say with dignity and composure. "If you're threatened by my presence, then perhaps you have something to hide."

Spencer's eyes narrow to slits. "Is that so?" he says in a growling whisper.

I make my gaze as hard as steel too. "That is so."

"Then maybe we can get together and have our own private interview."

My skin runs hot as I'm trapped by his carnal gaze. But something deep down inside says he doesn't mean it. He doesn't want to have sex. Spencer is toying with me. No, it's more than that— he's subtly and expertly, trivializing me and my work.

Bryn slaps the table. "Damn it, Spencer! Leave her alone!"

Suddenly, Jasper Blackstone in all his divineness strolls into the dining room as though he owns it.

Our gazes connect, at least for a few seconds, and I remember how it felt to be against him. I bashfully drop my gaze to the table.

"Why are you late?" Bryn snaps.

"I had business to attend to." Our eyes lock for a moment as he sits directly across from me, making my heart pound like thunder.

The doors to the kitchen open, and a man in a chef's coat and hat comes out, giving me a reason to keep my eyes off Jasper's perfect face. The chef announces that in the spirit of the season, we have been served sweet potato, ginger and turnip soup which will be followed by encrusted, pan-seared tuna drizzled with Riesling cream sauce on a bed of wild mushroom risotto.

Jasper thanks the chef and then glares at me just as the flavors of my first spoonful of soup spread throughout my mouth.

"I hope our guest has been on her best behavior," he says.

I want to shout, *what the hell is wrong with you people? Why are you all so paranoid?*

But before I can ask Jasper what the hell does he mean by that, Bryn, out of the blue, announces that she's hired me to do the initial fact-finding and information gathering for their family's official biography.

Looking as if his day has gotten horribly worse, Jasper's frown deepens. "Biography?"

"And before you get your boxers or briefs in a bunch, Randolph has not only approved the book, he signed the contract. He owes that to me, to us. Don't you think, Jasper?"Bryn holds a dare in her eyes.

And I have been stunned breathless. There's a deeper meaning behind what Bryn just asked Jasper and I can't help but wonder what that is.

"You know very well that Father..." Jasper hisses and then glances at me. "I'm the one who gives the approval."

Bryn shrugs indifferently and then digs into her soup. "It's done Jasper. Sue me."

I wait for Jasper to go ballistic because he seems like the type. Instead, he frowns at Bryn as if he thinks her behavior is treasonous and he can't quite figure out what to do about it.

"My secretary has sent a copy to each of your lawyers," Bryn says.

"What are you up to, Bryn?" Asher asks. I'm surprised he spoke at all. He and his girlfriend had been very quiet. But they've been more than just silent. It feels as if there's something heavy sitting between them.

Bryn's eyes are glossy when she looks at Asher and says, "I'm up to writing a simple book. I hired Holly because she's the best. You all should thank me, actually. She's fair, and only reports the facts." She sets her focus on Jasper. "Unless you're afraid of the facts."

"Don't," Asher warns and oddly Bryn's lips clamp as her back snaps against her chair.

I'm shocked by the level of power he has over her. She's been nothing short of a firecracker toward her eldest brother, or more like his rebellious child. However, it isn't until Asher speaks up does Bryn show any signs of backing down.

I get a sense that Asher could insist that Bryn put an end to her invasive project, and she will do it. But he doesn't want her to kill the project. And now it's him who's locking eyes with me. I suspect Asher knows that I know, I'm right.

"There'll be no book," Jasper insists. I rip my eyes off Asher and my attention lands on Jasper, who's watching me with that something extra in his eyes. "Miss Henderson can stay but…"

"Yes," Bryn says, cutting him off. "There will be

a book. And just so you know, this is my project. All research and the final manuscript will be given to me to publish. She's ghostwriting—for me. Right, Holly?"

I try to keep a straight face. That's news to me too. I'm Holly Henderson, awarding winning journalist, not a ghost writer. "Sure," I barely say. It's clear by my tone that I'm not committing to ghost writing Bryn's project. She and I will have to talk.

Asher's girlfriend sighs like she's bored. Then we're interrupted by servers who come out of the kitchen to collect our bowls and set the main course in front of us.

I take my first bite of tuna and the flavors saturate my mouth. *My goodness, where did this cook come from?*

"Then you want Holly Henderson to interview me?" Spencer asks, watching me with greedy eyes.

"Of course. I'm sure you have something you want to tell the world, especially about our mother," Bryn replies.

Spencer's handsome but cynical smirk goes bye-bye and now he almost looks as if he's swallowed a boulder and is choking on it.

I wonder what's behind the way blood has just drained from his face?

"There will be no goddamn interviews or biography," Jasper's voice booms causing me to snatch my focus off of Spencer and put it on him.

What is up with the Blackstones? Holy shit, I think I just landed in a den of snakes and secrets. My inner journalist can't help but wonder what the Blackstones are hiding.

A Phantom in the Night

HOLLY HENDERSON

We mostly eat in silence. Any conversation the siblings have is surface like the logistics of parking for the Christmas party and a boutique hotel in town that they are renting—wait—they own. They discuss which guests to house at that location and why. I listen for any names I recognize. So far, I identify four people. Two are politicians and two are philanthropists. I've already sussed out that the party being discussed is a donor money grab. Therefore, I practically tune out the rest of their conversation and focus on the food. The flavors of the main course are taking me straight to Heaven, but the others look as if they're stuck in hell on earth. I feel as though the family would have a more robust conversation if I were not at the table. I also feel as if Gina is more than just Asher's girlfriend. The others are too comfortable with her but not in a "she's merely an old friend" kind of way. I can't quite put my finger on the type of relationship that's between Gina and the family, but one certainly exists. Then when we are finished eating the delicious second course, Jasper announces that dinner has officially ended and the servants will bring dessert and a late-night bottle of wine to our rooms. He also informs his siblings that he will see them for breakfast in the morning. He turns to me and says, "Miss Henderson, your breakfast will be brought to your quarters."

My mouth falls open in shock. I don't know whether I should agree to that or not, but when I look at Bryn, she nods. Apparently, the Blackstones have to take care of some secret family business that more than likely has to do with me. For a moment, I consider sneaking downstairs tomorrow morning, post myself where I can't be seen, and listen to them. More than likely Jasper will have William posted outside my door.

When we all stand to leave, Jasper calls my name and then walks quickly over to me with a hand extended. "It was enjoyable having you join us for dinner tonight, Miss Henderson." He's still calling me Miss Henderson which means he still doesn't consider me a friend. So, I roll my eyes but shake his hand anyway. He captures my small hand in his much larger hand, puts his lips near my ear, and whispers, "Lock your door tonight."

My heart is beating a mile a minute as I watch Jasper walk away with the confidence of a king. I touch my ear. It's still warm from his breath.

Then, before Jasper and Spencer round the corner, Spencer turns around to wink at me.

"Do not have sex with him," Bryn says.

I jump slightly, unaware she's standing next to me. "Don't worry," I whisper.

"Not Spencer. Jasper."

She and I stare at each other. It's clear that she knows I have this odd attraction toward her extraordinarily handsome but dark brother.

"He'll break you into a million pieces," she warns.

———

HEAD DROPPED FORWARD, I MASSAGE MY TEMPLES, remembering Bryn's spur of the moment warning. I thought she didn't know whether or not Jasper prefers men over women. Her warning suggests that she does indeed know which sex her brother prefers and therefore, I should steer clear of him. But I'm not so sure she cautioned me because she's looking out for my well-being more than hers.

I can't work with Bryn if she willfully continues to lie to me. Or maybe my curiosity has driven me far beyond all the crap Bryn sprung on me at the dinner table. She wants me to be her ghostwriter? Ha! Never. I will be her investigator, though. I will get to the bottom of all the secrets the Blackstones are hiding. And as a tradeoff I will keep the secret about Randolph upstairs in his sickbed private.

———

WHEN I MAKE IT BACK TO MY BEDROOM, I continue to ponder Jasper's secret warning. Why would he tell me to lock my door? Regardless of the fact that his brothers don't want me here, they seem harmless enough. Jasper sure isn't warning me against Bryn. But I lock the door before stripping off my dress, washing my makeup off my face, and slipping into an over-sized nightshirt. The temperature of the room is warm but there are certain parts that feel drafty, like right here, beside the standing mirror.

There's a knock on my door, and a female's voice announces dessert. I dash out of the bath-room to let her in. If dessert is half as good as dinner, then I'm certainly in for the experience of a lifetime.

A woman wearing a chef's jacket brings in a dessert tray and two men setup a larger table over the small round table that's normally set between the two high-backed chairs. The crew cap off their service by setting a beautiful gold wine bucket in the center of the table that holds an open bottle of Chablis. I've been instructed to ring the kitchen once I'm done eating and drinking.

Despite Bryn's odd brothers, I'm loving every moment of being a guest in the Blackstone family mansion. The food is good. The desserts are mouthwatering and decadent. My bath was perfect too. I fire up my laptop, connect to my hotspot, and search the news databases to which I have access. I find as many articles as I can about the Blackstones. As I read, I take my time devouring the treats, which include mini chocolate cakes filled with creamy custards and whipped mousses, tarts of all flavors, and light as air cream cheese pies.

Time flies by. When I give into the fact that there is hardly any negative press on the Blackstones to discover, only a little more than half a bottle of wine is left, and most of my desserts have been consumed. I rub my full belly. I think I may have overdone it in the eating department today. If tonight's dinner is any indication of what the rest of the meals are going to be like, then I think I might gain a good five to ten pounds during my short visit.

I sigh as I close my laptop and yawn. The two full glasses of wine that I drank have made me dizzy and sleepy. I call for the servants to collect the dessert trays which they do in record time. I don't forget to lock the door behind me. After brushing my teeth, I turn off the lights, and climb into the very comfortable bed which instantly relaxes me. Soon, I'm sleeping.

I GROAN, WONDERING IF I'M DREAMING. IS IT A ghost whispering my name.

"Miss Henderson," a man's voice calls.

The ghost that would haunt this room will more than likely be a woman, not a man.

I slowly open my eyes and let my sight adjust to

the darkness. Then my heart nearly stops as I clench a hand over my chest and gasp. It's not a ghost. It's a real life human being, a man. Panicked, I quickly sit up and pitch my back against the luxurious headboard.

"It's me, Jasper," the man whispers.

I reach over to turn on the lamp sitting on top of the nightstand. My eyes expand. "What are you doing here?"

"Should I leave?" he whispers.

I focus on the fire in his eyes. He's shirtless, and the ripples of his abs and hills and crests of his chest make his body look as if it's carved of limestone.

But still he's slightly out of focus so I rub my eyes. "I don't know," I answer honestly.

"Holly," he says in a commanding whisper. "Do you want me to go?"

I blink at his sexy face. No man has the features of Jasper Blackstone. His forehead is straight, jaw chiseled and he has that sexy dimple in his chin. His lips are sensual, kissable. He reminds me of a wild warrior of ancient times, only he's been tamed, trimmed, and scrubbed.

Then my gaze drops to his lower half. Jasper is wearing loose-fitting pajama bottoms, and his full-blown erection pokes the material. My chest tightens. My lust sizzle. It seems Mr. Blackstone has made a calculated guess regarding my desire for him, or else he wouldn't be standing in my room beside my bed with a massive erection.

"But how did you get in here?" I ask as I look around the room, trying to find an entrance. "Do you have a key?"

"Yes. But I didn't use a key," he replies rather impatiently. His eyes burn with more lust. "Holly. You haven't answered my question. Do you want me to leave?"

I press my lips as saliva pours into my mouth. I shake my head as I swallow. "No," I barely say.

"Then stand up," he says.

I hesitate, wondering, is this really happening. This moment seems so unreal. But his rippling abs, hard chest and that face that can stop air traffic makes me push the covers off of me and stand to my feet. We're face to face, and without delay Jasper takes the hem of my shirt and pulls it over my head. The next thing I feel is warm wetness covering one of my nipples, making me moan and tremble down below. Then I feel teeth. My head drops back, and I cry out at the soft ache of his bite then the soothing warmth of his sucking and licking.

He does the same thing to my other nipple as a number of his fingers slide up and down my slit, steadily rubbing my clit until my legs wobble and I wrap my arms around him to stop myself from dropping onto the bed.

Jasper holds me against him. His mouth is against my temple.

"Holly. I want this between us while you're here. I don't do this ever, but there's something about you. I must have you. Please let me have you," he whispers.

His hardness against me... His warmth too... And I am an adult. And this can and will get complicated between us. But, I can hardly breathe because I want him so badly.

And so, I whisper, "Yes. You can have me."

Suddenly, Jasper steps back to get an eyeful of my nakedness. "Damn, you're so beautiful," he whispers thickly.

The next thing I know, I'm on the bed with my back against the mattress, and his face is between my thighs. My hazy gaze watches the top of his head as Jasper stimulates me, making noises as though he loves how I taste. All the sensations stirring inside of me are so potent as I claw at the bedding. Pleasure builds like an inferno, promising an explosion that will shoot me to the moon.

I cry out his name and call on the Almighty as my orgasm builds and climbs.

His fingers grip me tightly so my hips can't escape his pleasurable assault. Sucking air, I search for something steadier to hold on to. The bed sheets will no longer suffice. His hair feels too soft.

"Oh, Jasper," are the last intelligible words I speak before the deepest, most intense orgasm ever gusts through me. I scream and cry as he somehow makes it last longer, his tongue works slowly but steadily while the sensations ease.

"I've been wanting to do that since I first saw you," he says as he stands to take off his pajama bottoms. "Do not close your legs," he commands while staring at my slit.

My eyes expand at the girth and length of his rock-hard cock. He's already wearing a condom. He came into my room knowing exactly what he wanted to do to me. That's sensually hot.

Then, he's on top of me.

I cry out with pleasure as he slams inside me. I can feel every bit of him, engorged inside me.

Jasper breathes heavily as he thrusts into me

harder and harder. He's hungry, starving, pumping into me as if our survival depends on it.

And then, "No," he says in a shivering voice as he stuffs his manhood deep inside me and holds steady. "Not yet. You feel too good."

With his heaviness upon me, I'm experiencing sensory overload. It's still so surreal that Jasper Blackstone is inside me like this. I want to rub his back, but I don't want to confuse what we're doing with true affection. No. This is raw, animalistic, expression of lust we're banging out right now. This is the result of hours of sexual tension which started from the moment he knocked on my window, stepped back and I got a really good look at him.

Our gazes meet. Slowly, Jasper tries pumping into me again. Each thrust is careful, in and out. His hips shift, and his eyes close then open. He looks as if he's on some magnificent drugs.

"Oh," he mutters, his mouth next to my ear. Then our mouths melt and he leads us in a deep, hot, and delicious kiss.

Damn…

My hips ride up to meet his and that seems to make him lose control. Deeply, indulgently Jasper thrusts into me. My moan is so telling as he increases the speed of his prodding. He moves quicker and quicker as I moan and pant, and…

"Ah," I cry out, clinging to him for dear life. My eyes widen in disbelief as I come, hard.

Then Jasper grunts. His lower half jerks, and his body shivers. He holds me so close while coming that I can hardly breathe.

———

ONCE JASPER STILLS, HE CONTINUES LYING ON TOP of me. His heaviness is so that I want him to fall into me and merge with my soul. I don't move a muscle because I can already feel that he will soon leave. I already know that Jasper Blackstone is not the sort of man who sticks around to cuddle a woman after screwing her. He isn't going to sleep next to me for a while, allowing his body to grow a brand-new erection so we can do it all over again, and again, and again.

Finally, Jasper kisses me again, deeply and greedily. I am famished for him, so I match his intensity. He sucks my neck, and I suck his. We bite and claw at each other. I want to break into his skin, consume him, and he wants to do the same to me. I just know it.

Then, all of a sudden, Jasper rolls off me. "We'll do this again, soon."

I watch in a daze as he pulls his pants back on, turns his back on me, and opens the large, decorative wardrobe closet that I'd thought was too lavish to do anything but be admired. Then he disappears inside the wardrobe and closes the door behind him.

I sit up. "What…?" That's a secret door leading right into my guest room

Round Two

HOLLY HENDERSON

DECEMBER 22ND

The alarm on my cell phone is blasting. It must be six a.m. It's set to go off every morning at this time. I forgot to tell it that I'm on a mini-break. Regardless, I slowly rise and shine, rubbing my eyes as I sit up. Seated against the headboard, I stare at the wardrobe against the wall near the window. My heart races. I press my thighs together and feel shadows of the sex I had during the wee hours of the morning with Jasper Blackstone.

I slap a hand over my mouth. "Oh no."

But oh yes, we did it.

I close my eyes to sigh with dread and longing. I

also remember that he had proposed some sort of sex deal between us. While I'm here, we screw. When I leave the nature of our association will end. I said yes. It's not too late to back out but I don't want to. I want Jasper Blackstone. I reach over to finally turn off my alarm and while stretching my body and extending my arm, I admit that I want him right now.

LAST NIGHT I WAS CAUGHT IN A STRANGE STATE OF euphoria that stemmed from the stressful dinner with the family, the good food, fast wine, and then sex. Today, I'm more levelheaded, and still so very confused about the real reason why I'm here. During my first one on one with Bryn, I thought she steered me into believing that I'm here to find out why Amelia Blackstone felt as though she hadn't needed to apologize for being a bad mother. I still haven't questioned Bryn about what in particular made Amelia such a bad mother. But then at dinner she said she wants me to ghostwrite the family's autobiography. Well, that's not such a simple project.

Before I move on with my day, I definitely

should have a talk with her first. That will deter-
mine how I use my time during my visit.

I could definitely slide back into bed and sleep
for a few more hours, but not yet. I need to know
more. It's still too early to seek out Bryn. So I decide
to take a long warm shower and then really spend
time on making my face look extra pretty which is
definitely a change from yesterday. When I left my
apartment in Philadelphia, I didn't even put on
makeup. That means Jasper had been attracted to
makeup-less me.

I grunt, intrigued. *That's interesting.*

However, after a light dusting of red lipstick,
eyeliner and mascara, I put on a warm pair of black
jeans, a black boat-neck sweater, and faux-fur lined
ankle boots to keep my feet warm on a snowy day.
Since it's finally after seven a.m., I slide into my
black wool trench coat and head out to look for
Bryn's room.

"Oh," I say as I jump. William is posted outside
my door as I guessed he would be.

It seems one sexual encounter is not enough to
win Jasper's trust. As a matter of fact, he probably
trusts me less. He might think I'll use sex to control
him. And I sure as hell know he'll use it to control
me. I have to keep my wits about me.

"Good morning, Miss Henderson. Are you ready for breakfast in your room?"

A cynical snort escapes me. *Oh… Jasper. You are something else.* I really shouldn't have sex with him again.

"Um no, William." I frown curiously. "Where can I find Bryn's room?"

He hesitates. Behind his eyes I can tell that he's trying to figure out if he should deviate from the orders he's been given while serving me well as my butler.

"I really need to speak to her," I add.

Finally, William nods sharply. "Follow me, please."

Oddly, Bryn's room is on the first floor. I guessed that all family bedrooms are on the third floor where Randolph is resting. I sure would love to get a look at him. However, that's going to be hard to accomplish with William glued to my side.

Bryn's bedroom is near a side exit that is the smallest door I've seen in this house. The longer I look at the unremarkable and newer wood, the more I can see that it's a more modern addition. I grunt thoughtfully. I don't know why seeing the door feels so significant, it just does.

William waits while I knock. There's no shaking

him it seems. I hear no sound inside Bryn's room so I knock harder and then call her name.

Pressing my lips, I turn to William. My eyebrows pull.

"Are you my prison guard?" I ask.

"No, Miss Henderson," he says in a dull voice.

I tilt my head. "Then I can dismiss you and you will go."

"Yes, Miss Henderson."

I shake my head like it's a rattle. "Then, please. You may go. You're being dismissed."

William bows smoothly and I watch as he composedly walks toward the inner part of the home. I don't take my eyes off of him until he's out of sight. I knock on Bryn's door again. This time I'm louder when I call her name.

Still, there's no reply.

I twist the knob and it doesn't budge. The door is locked. *Hmm...*

I glare down the hallway. I'm certain William has positioned himself strategically to intercept me. Now that I haven't had the opportunity to chat with Bryn, I really need to be at the breakfast table this morning. So, instead of heading back in the direction from where I came, I walk out into the crisp morning.

The cold and fog makes me hug myself and shiver. But I do not let the temperature deter me. I grab the lapels of my coat so that chilly air can't travel down my bosom. I pad down a short set of stairs, and just walk.

JASPER BLACKSTONE

I leave the guesthouse and head to the main house. This is where I sleep. I refuse to sleep in the cursed monstrosity called the home I grew up in. I sniff in the cold fog, even though it's beginning to lift, the vapors freeze my brain enough to take thoughts of her, Holly Henderson, away from me. Walking between the trees and gazing up at the mansion that looms in the distance reminds me of how much I hate this place. I have been living in Southern California for the past four months, near the beach. It's going to be seventy-eight degrees in LA today. When I woke up yesterday morning, I wished I was there. This morning, I'm where I want to be, especially after what happened in Amelia's room.

Holly Henderson.

Why does she drive me mad with lust? I

should've been there when she woke up this morning. I want to be inside her right now. But I must delay our next encounter. I have other things to think about like my father.

The thought of seeing Randolph makes each step through the cold morning a chore. My father isn't a saint. He isn't a sinner either. He's the devil incarnate. Throughout my life he'd been loyal to no one but required devotion from everyone.

He's committed dastardly acts in his lifetime. God help me, I covered up a lot of them for the sake of my siblings and my mother. When Randolph suffered his first major stroke three years ago, he lost the ability to speak and care for himself. He has a full-time staff that sees to his daily needs. However, when poor health took my father out of commission, I never felt freer.

Do I love the man? I used to. Over the many years of getting a front row seat to his corroded soul, my love has turned to pure hatred. Especially for what he did to Amelia.

But I have changed everything. I fired his accountants and lawyers. I've also been avoiding Arthur Valentine, his partner in crime. I have to figure out what the hell to do about Valentine. He still has his hooks in my family. Arthur is the only person in the world Randolph jumped through hoops for. Randolph always said we owe a lot to the Valentines. When I asked him to elaborate, he chose not to. I had combed the books dozens of times, trying to find any payments from Valentine Corp. or any of its subsidiaries, but I never found a thing. That means our debt to the Valentines has something to do with the dark forces that work within my father, and that makes Arthur Valentine a very dangerous man.

I stop in my tracks, and so does she. Out of the vapors comes Holly Henderson. I'm looking at her, and it's so damn unreal. It has been years since a woman has activated dormant parts of me. But she does it for me. And I'm ready… I lick my lips. I'm so damn ready.

HOLLY HENDERSON

"Hi." The word is barely able to escape my tight throat.

He doesn't say hello back. Instead, Jasper is staring at me with the same fire in his eyes that I've seen so often from him.

"Follow me," he says and starts walking in the direction from where he came.

He's very confident in the fact that I will follow. And he's right to have that confidence. My body is reeling for his touch. Without much effort from my brain to stop my feet from obeying Jasper Blackstone, I walk where he leads.

He's slowed his pace so that I can shuffle alongside him. Every now and then we will glance at each other. The desire between us is all too consuming for us to talk. Every inch of me craves his touch. If Jasper threw me down on top of the cobblestone path we're traveling on, I would let him. If he ripped me out of my clothes so that the elements could freeze my skin, bent me over the well-groomed bushes that line this quaint path, and slammed himself inside me, I would let him.

"How did you sleep?" he finally asks, gaze pointed forward.

Up ahead to our right I see a stone craftsman cottage. Smoke snakes up from the chimney.

"Fine, and you?" I finally say as Jasper leads me to the door.

He turns the knob and holds the door open for me to enter. "I'm doing a lot better now," he says.

One corner of his mouth lifts into the sexiest

smile ever. I want to kiss him. But I'm not so sure if I should ever take the lead with him during this brief affair of ours. That's a recipe for getting addicted to something that I will no longer be able to have in five more days.

"So is this where you're sleeping?" I ask as I walk in. The warmth in the air begins to defrost my frozen blood.

Earlier, I saw a man through the thick vapors of fog from a distance. I knew it was Jasper because of his height and that regal way that he carries himself. Before I laid eyes on him, I was on the verge of running back to the manor as fast as I could. The cold was getting the better of me. But instead of retreating to the warmth of my bedroom, I approached him. He probably wouldn't have seen me if I hadn't.

The door closes. Then almost as quick as a lightning strike my back is against wood, and Jasper is tonguing me. Our tongues and lips never let go of each other as he undoes my jeans then shoves his hand down my pants and stimulates me with his insatiable fingers.

My head spins as my greed matches his. It's all so insane, this unquenchable lust we have for each other. He said he doesn't do this often, but I don't believe him, and I don't care.

Jasper forces his mouth away from mine. Breathing heavily, he closes his eyes and presses his thumbs against his temples. "What are you doing to me?"

I raise my eyebrows while dropping my head to look at the floor. "What are you doing to *me*?" I mutter.

I look up. We're staring at each other, really getting a good look at each other. My breaths come heavier and so do his.

Jasper moves towards me.

My feet are swept off the floor, and we make out feverishly as he carries me. I get the sense that we're passing through a dim hallway only lit by gray daylight. His mouth tastes so good. We moan together. I press against him, squirming with need in his arms.

Jasper brings me into a bedroom made comfortable by flames brewing in the fireplace. He lays me on top of a large king-sized bed.

"Don't move," he whispers lustfully.

He carefully takes off my boots, my socks, and slides off my pants. Then, almost indulgently he takes my panties by the side. Staring at my crotch, he licks his lips. Knowing what will soon come makes me wetter. Slowly he slides them down my legs. My sex throbs for his touch.

"Umm," we moan together as his fingers slip in and out of my wetness until his thumb rounds my clit.

He's trying to get me off, and I toss my head back and gasp because that's exactly what he's doing—getting me off.

"I'm coming," I whimper, clawing at the messy blankets. This is where Jasper slept last night. I can smell him on the linens.

Then, suddenly, a warm silky mouth takes over where his fingers left off, leaving me floating on a cloud of pure pleasure.

His mouth feels so supple on my clit. *Sigh…* I arch my back and angle my hips toward his mouth and try to retract when the pleasure becomes all too consuming. But I can't move an inch away from what he's doing to me. Just as it was in the wee hours of the morning when Jasper first went down on me, he has my buttocks in a grip that I can't escape.

So I cry out, suck air and then, "Ah!" My sex convulses and my legs jump because I climax so hard.

"You taste so good," he whispers as he gets to his feet.

I roll onto my side and curl up. My orgasm hasn't finished dwindling.

"You're good at that," I say.

He glances over his shoulder at me with his eyebrows up as he opens a drawer belonging to a large dresser. Jasper takes off his off-white sweater, and then the T-shirt underneath. The rippling muscles in his back make my mouth water. I can't wait to slide my hands up and down them. I can't wait to feel his heaviness on top of me. He steps out of his pants. *What a perfect derriere he has.* Then a condom wrapper rips open. I can tell he's sliding it on.

"Are you on the pill?" he asks.

I wish I were. "No."

"I need you on the pill because I want to feel you." He turns around, and his massive erection is facing me.

I don't know what to say to that. "I'll be gone in five days, so…"

He cracks a tiny smile as he walks toward me. He's holding his cock the way a man does when he's preparing to enter wetness. "Then when was your last period?" He opens my thighs wider. I fall back on the bed as he moves inside me and sucks air.

My moan is indicative of how good he feels, stretching me, filling me.

"When?" he demands as he pumps in and out of my moisture.

Each thrust of his gorgeous cock feels so damn good. I can't believe he wants to have this discussion right now.

Oh… "I can't remember," I say breathlessly.

"Try." He rolls me on top of him, grips my buttocks and shifts me harder against his length. Jasper closes his eyes, and the look on his face makes me believe he's experiencing the most pleasurable feeling of his life.

"Oh…" he says as I shove my hips so hard against him that I can feel him deep in my belly. He rolls himself back on top of me. His eyes are still closed, and he remains motionless, gnawing on his bottom lip as though he's trying to contain himself. "You're too tight."

And he's too thick, so much so that I feel corked by his expansive girth. Then I remember something. "My period was on the twelfth of this month."

He curses under his breath then stares into my eyes. "I shouldn't be doing this with you."

"I agree," I whisper.

"I can't stop wanting you, though."

"Me neither," I confess.

We stare at each other for a long time. Then, almost on cue we chuckle together. I know why I'm laughing and I think he's doing it for the same reason. We've lost our minds. I know for certain that Jasper Blackstone is a sensible man. Well, I'm a sensible woman. But look at us. We're not behaving so sensibly.

Jasper slowly starts shifting his cock in and out of me again. Gently, his lips find mine, and we kiss. Our pace is slow as he moves deeper inside me.

He feels so damn good and I let him hear it.

Then, Jasper grunts as his entire body quakes until he stills.

My arms around him, my hands sliding up and down his muscular back, I wish we could stay like this forever.

Then, he kisses me on the cheek. "Sorry, Beautiful. I wanted to last for you."

He wanted to last for me?

"Jasper?" I say.

"Yes," he replies.

"Could you look at me?"

It takes him a moment, but he does it, although he's frowning intensely.

"So this is what we have? Just sex?"

"I can't give you more," he whispers.

I roll my eyes as if that's obvious. "I know that."

He yanks his head back. "You do?"

"I do."

"Why is that?"

I gnaw on my lower lip, wondering if I should tell the truth. Then, my lower lip is inside Jasper's warm mouth and his soft tongue is stroking it.

"I...damn it. I wish I didn't come so fast," he whispers.

I don't know what to say to that.

"But you still haven't answered my question," he says.

I close my eyes. "Why do you even care what I think anyway? After all, we're just fucking."

"Because you're brilliant, Holly Henderson."

I narrow an eye curiously. "How do you know I'm brilliant?"

"I've read your books. And I know your reputation."

My eyebrows flash up as I study his face. I have

no idea what I'm searching for—maybe signs that I should watch my back.

"I know your reputation too," I finally say.

He smirks as if pleased by that. "I want you again Holly Henderson—today."

"Then I'm your friend?" I say.

He looks confounded.

"You said you only call your friends by their first names. But last night and today, you've been calling me by my first name."

Jasper grunts thoughtfully. "Then I guess we are friends."

I press my lips, contemplatively. He's staring at my face as if he's waiting for me to say something. How intuitive of him, I do have something to say.

"Are you trying to sex me into not working with Bryn?" I finally ask.

Jasper arches an eyebrow. "Is it working."

My eyes expand in shock until he laughs.

"If it's working, then yes. If not, then no," he says as he carefully takes himself out of me.

"That's a puzzle for the record books," I say, rolling onto my side and propping my head up with my palm.

Jasper winks at me and then rolls off the bed. Very quickly he's dressing himself. I can tell that his mood has shifted too. He's no longer the smirking and grinning Jasper, who just made two jokes. His face is serious again as he zips up his pants and then goes to the bathroom.

I feel as if I should be getting dressed too. However, I'm frozen in a state of not knowing what to do next.

He's back and he puts on his T-shirt. "You should get back to the house." Then he quickly puts on his sweater and then shoes. "Close the door on your way out."

He turns around to look at me. His lustful gaze runs up and down my naked body. A breath catches in my chest as my desire purrs. The need in his eyes is almost too much for me to bear. And then, without another word, he leaves me alone.

Sick Bed

JASPER WALKER BLACKSTONE

A s soon as I walk in through the back door, Nigel, the house butler, takes my coat. "Good morning, Jasper. Breakfast will be served in half an hour." Then he hands me the *Times*.

I inhale slowly, indiscernibly. I still smell her pussy on my face—taste her in my mouth.

I take the newspaper from him. "Is Father improving?"

"No, he's not. He's taken a turn for the worse overnight. I didn't inform you because you asked—"

I raise a hand to stop him from saying it. "I know what I asked. That's fine."

I look up the curved stairway. Randolph's

room is on the third floor, and these days he rarely leaves it. *A turn for the worse?* He's already on his last leg. However, I was happy Nigel hadn't disturbed me. I had plans to make love to Holly Henderson all night long. I wanted to do her until she couldn't stand. I wanted to drink all the juices she had to offer. I wanted to fuck her out of my system, and be done with her. But my plans were being thwarted, and it started the second I went down on her. Her puffy, delectable slit that my mouth found tantalizing... That intoxicated look in her eyes as my tongue stroked her clit... The heat from her inner thighs warming my face... Then she came, and that made her wetter. I fucked her like a madman. I never do it that way. I can't get enough of Holly Henderson. Already, I want her again.

The way we kiss... What the hell was that my heart felt? Why do I want to hold her against me and grind her until I'm ready for the next round? I want to flip her on her back and suck her nipples, bite them and taste the supple flesh around them until they are sore. I want to devour her, eat her alive. I want her to tell me her plans for the next five to ten years just so I can demand that she casts them aside. I will be her new plan. Every part of her will belong to me—her heart, her mind, and her soft, puffy slit.

I set my focus back on Nigel, making sure he doesn't see anything in my expression that will expose the thoughts I'm having about our house guest. "I'll go up now."

I take my time climbing the stairs. I probably should've asked Nigel how bad off Father is. He won't share those kinds of details without my asking. Nigel is the best butler money can buy. He's been around a long time. He knows where all the bodies are buried, and even so, my father can hardly remember Nigel's last name. "It's Farmington, you asshole," I shout at my father in my head. My father has also put together a crafty retirement package for Nigel in which payments will stop abruptly if the butler discloses any of my father's indiscretions. But Nigel has been around Randolph Blackstone long enough to know that there's an unwritten stipulation in his contract, one that puts him six feet under if he talks to the wrong people. Thinking about that threat lording over Nigel makes me shudder. I will never let anything bad happen to the man I owe everything to. I'd kill Randolph before I let him get his hands on our butler.

I make it to my father's quarters and brace myself as I put my hand around the fine brass doorknob. Usually the door is locked, but Nigel made sure the hospice care staff kept it unlocked for my arrival. *No more stalling.* I enter.

The room covers half the third floor. My father expanded it after Amelia abandoned it. I was in high school then. The two never explained why they decided to sleep in separate bedrooms. But one day I discovered why.

I pad through my father's personal parlor. The brown leather furniture is polished. He use to entertain some of the most powerful men in the country in this space, treating them to cigars, alcohol, cocaine, and high-end prostitutes, male or female, depending on a man's preference.

I release my breath after clearing that space and enter his bedroom. There are no more prostitutes sitting on his limp cock, trying to keep it up. He's alone and is as pale as a ghost with tubes hooked up to his body and a breathing apparatus over his mouth. Up until his last major stroke, he could write out his orders on a chalkboard with a shaky hand. Not anymore though. I won't be purchasing sixteen local television stations so his snaky political allies can pump false information to an unsuspecting public. I also, won't be inviting Cornelius Dugan to our annual Christmas party. Dugan is a political strategist who will crawl under the lowest bar on the planet to win an election. I don't like the guy. I don't respect the guy. He wears his soul in his appearance—brown teeth, puffy skin, and sunken eyes. Even though he could hardly walk or talk before he took a turn for the worse, Randolph still entertained visits from his cronies just so they could kiss his ring. By the looks of it, Randolph Wesley Blackstone is in no shape to entertain Dugan. I'll have Stephanie, my personal assistant, disinvite him. I don't want him slithering his way onto the property, not while Holly Henderson is here. She'll know who he is. And I don't want her to think Blackstone Family Enterprises is associated with that gutter mite.

I didn't notice the nurse standing at attention, watching me as I examine my father.

"Good morning, Laura," I say to the exhausted-looking woman in the blue hospital scrubs.

"Good morning, Jasper," she says with a sigh.

I turn my gaze back on my dying father. "So what happened to him?"

She walks over to stand on the other side of his bed, picks up his chart, and starts reading.

"Through the night, he suffered a series of small strokes. But he's finally stabilized."

"I see. Is Dr. Caro around?"

"I'm here," the doctor says.

Then, Dr. Caro walks into the room and provides me the full prognosis in regard to Randolph's recovery.

It's after eight a.m., and my siblings and I, as well as Gina, are seated at the table, eating breakfast. I tell them what Dr. Caro told me. The mood is somber but not because we're sad. Our lives are on the verge of changing for the better, and we knew it. There are a few slithery characters that won't go away so easily, but I can handle them. I'll have fun destroying each and every one of them. *But what will it be like not to live under Randolph Blackstone's watchful eye?*

I see the way Asher, Spencer, and Bronwyn are watching me. I can see the question in their eyes. They're wondering if I will become him. They should know better. All operations are going to run better with me at the helm—business and family. I'm better at maintaining control of the family fortune than my father, and my pinkie finger is smarter than his brain. Because Randolph lived his whole life feeding his addiction. I've never been addicted to anything, that's until Holly Henderson showed up.

"Then he *is* dying?" Asher asks, dipping his chin, eyebrows raised curiously.

There's no reason to sugarcoat the truth. "So it seems."

"Then what do you want from us?" Bryn snaps. "He's dying. So what?"

I mean for my scowl to burn the hell out of her. Bryn is a brat, and even more so now that she's twenty-seven and committed to nothing and nobody. But it's not her fault. Randolph cut her off from having any hopes or dreams beyond landing an advantageous marriage. But unlike Randolph, I know that Bryn will kill herself before she commits to a man she doesn't love. And she really would kill herself which is why she's spent most of her life waiting to die.

"It's more of a matter of what I need from you," I say to her.

"If you're referring to the book, you can't stop this train, Ace. It's still a go." She sets her jaw defiantly.

I hoist my body toward her. "Don't fucking test me, Bryn. You might not like the results."

She snaps back in her chair. "Are you threatening me?"

I sigh forcefully. She of all people knows I don't make threats. "No."

"Good. Because legally, you can't stop this book. Try to stop me, and I will…"

We wait for her to finish her statement, but instead, she shakes her head like a petulant five-year-old.

"You'll what?" Spencer asks.

She drops her head. "I don't know. Just… I don't know." She sounds as if she's on the verge of crying.

I know what she will do—nothing. She will never hurt any of us, which is why I'm surprised she wants Holly Henderson, the person who took down the Howsleys, to write our family's biography.

Everyone falls silent.

I study Bryn. She's become more fragile in recent years. She's sneaking around with Dale Rumor, planning her escape. I'm not going to hurt my sister if she crosses me. The best move I can make is to control her project.

"I want to see her notes," I say. "I want to know

who she's going to interview, when she's going to have her interviews, what questions she's going to ask, and how she's going to ask them."

Bryn folds her arms on her chest. "You'll see her notes, but that's it." Then she sets her hands on the table and leans toward me. "You're going to have to trust me on this, Jasper. This is my project, my contribution to the family. I'll never destroy us." She snarls as her eyes veer up and she nods toward the ceiling. "Especially if he's dead."

"Good morning." The voice instantly makes my dick start to grow.

"I invited Holls to join us for breakfast," Bryn says.

"So I'm here," Holly sings, avoiding eye contact with me.

I'm lost for words. First and foremost, Holly Henderson's skin glows, which I'd like to take credit for. Her dark hair is bouncy. I can smell her sweet shampoo and that other scent, that goddamn other scent she wears. *What is it?* My gaze veers down to her long legs clad in black pants and then up to her sweater that fits her sexy body like a glove. She hasn't changed clothes. Damn, will I have fun peeling her out of all that material. How dare she stroll into breakfast against my orders, looking that way? Then she sits next to Bryn. Her skin burns red as she finally and shyly glances at me.

She takes a nervous breath. "Um, so…" she starts and then stops to look at me with wide, unsure eyes. I'm happy she gets the message my glower is conveying. "This morning, Bryn and I discussed my approach to gathering the information for her book. You can rest easy because I will not ghostwrite her book, but I will gather information for her to give her ghostwriter." She looks at me. I glare at her. *I'm going to fuck the living daylights out of you, Holly Henderson.* Holly clears her throat. "Bryn, however, did provide stipulations regarding what areas of the Blackstones I could broach and which I could not."

"And which areas are those?" I ask.

"Any information regarding Randolph Blackstone's business partners and political allies. I would have to gain clearance from—"

"Me," I interrupt.

"Me," Bryn says.

I have to take a beat. "Do you think I can't nip your little project in the bud with one phone call?" My skin is hot, at the moment, and it's something I've never felt before, I'm ready to destroy my little sister if need be. I think it's because she's defying me in front of Holly. I care how Holly sees me. *Shit.*

And Bryn must've seen the truth in my eyes, because she clears her throat and says, "Okay. She'll report to the both of us."

"Me," I persist. "Only me."

After a beat, Bryn nods tightly.

"Good." I pick up the silver bell and ring to have breakfast served.

I steal a glance at Holly Henderson. She's studying me as if she sees the real me, the part of me that Randolph Blackstone has made, and it scares the hell out of her.

Breakfast with the Blackstone

HOLLY HENDERSON

What sort of insanity has Bryn put me in the middle of? Jasper looked at his little sister as if he wanted to rip her head off. And sure enough, Bryn received the message loud and clear. My heart beats out of my chest. I should be afraid too, but I'm not. I'm not afraid of anything. That's how *my* parents raised me.

"I don't mind reporting to all of you, actually," I say, hoping to take the sting out of the air. "This is your project, not mine. However, I'll tell you when we're on the record, and by the way, we're on the record." I mistakenly wink at Jasper. I hope no one saw that.

"Then, I'll go first," Spencer says, stealing my

attention away from his brother. He's stroking his chin, watching me as if he wants me just as much as Jasper does.

My eyebrows flash up as I seem to be drawn into Spencer's hypnotic eyes. It's as if he's trying to tell me something, actually he's saying a lot.

"I'm not hungry," Gina announces.

Finally Spencer's eyes release me to watch her walk out in a huff. Then, he and Asher lock eyes like rams lock horns. *What in the world is going on in these parts?* It'll be my job to find out.

"Do you think this is a game, Spence?" Jasper points a hand at me. "Have you ever heard of her?"

My chest tightens.

"I'm not the one who has to run for president," Spencer replies.

Has to? Something tells me that Spencer dropped that nugget on purpose. Spencer Blackstone runs a huge financial corporation and does so quite successfully. A man like him isn't as glib as he presents himself to be.

Jasper sets his dark eyes on me. "You don't interview him without my being there. You got that?"

Narrowing an eye, I tilt my head to the side. "What are you hiding?"

"What are you looking for?" The heat in his eyes sends sparks through my body.

"It depends on what you're covering up."

Silence that can't be cut with a chainsaw looms.

"Okay…" Bryn says, her voice ringing with a questioning tone.

Jasper's intense eyes burn through me. "You talk to me first, after breakfast. And as I said, you only talk to the others if I'm in the room."

I gulp as I visualize just how that talk is going to unfold. I can't speak; all I can do is nod.

"Here's one for you to figure out, Holly," Asher says. I'm surprised he's speaking to me, he's been so quiet. But there's a certain energy in his voice, and then he glares at Spencer. "In our family, we have a brother who crosses lines."

The only time I've seen Spencer look so angry is when Jasper showed up late for dinner last night.

"Quiet, Ash. This is not the time or place," he says with clenched lips.

"It really isn't," Jasper growls at Asher.

Asher snorts bitterly and then stands. He throws accusatory looks at both of his brothers, a final glance at Bryn, and then he walks out of the dining room with Gina following closely behind him.

Two down. The remaining siblings fall deadly

silent. There's one thing for sure, the rumor is true, Jasper Blackstone is the Blackstone family's puppet master.

FINALLY, THE FOOD SERVICE BEGINS. THE CHEF announces a breakfast of eggs Benedict with sweet Christmas ham, oven-roasted garlic potatoes, country butter, and cheese biscuits.

I can't believe Jasper wanted me to miss eating this breakfast at the table. My mouth waters as the servers set one of the plates before me. Is this how ultra-rich people eat? Every morning, I make myself oatmeal with apples, pecans, cinnamon and honey for breakfast. My usual is indeed healthier, but I would toss my oatmeal straight down the garbage chute if I had the option to eat like this every morning.

The first thing I bite into is the biscuit because it smells so divine.

"Are you enjoying your meal, Miss Henderson?" Jasper asks.

Spencer and Bryn chuckle.

I didn't realize my eyes were closed until he spoke. I open them, still chewing. "Umm… yes."

He nods sharply then looks down at his plate and clears his throat. "Good."

"A woman that's not afraid to eat." Spencer raises his eyebrows appreciatively.

I swallow the delicious food in my mouth, choosing to ignore the chronic Flirt. Spencer is very good-looking, though. But I made my choice. It's too late to switch up. So, I focus on the easiest interviewee at the table. "Here's what I would like to know," I say to Bryn. "What are you doing these days?" I asked her that question already, which she expertly evaded. But this time I'm hoping she'll say more now that we are seated with her brothers.

Her smile wavers. "What do you mean?"

"You never returned to Redmond College after our first year, and you never said why."

"She was expelled for cheating," Jasper replies. His words sound like the most practiced answer I ever heard.

"I see," I say, keeping my attention on Bryn. "Did you finish up somewhere else?"

Bryn presses a hand over her heart. "Oh, so I'm first?"

"Why not? Maybe we can help the others see that talking to me will only help, not hurt."

"It doesn't feel like you're helping me at all," she hisses.

I sit up straight. "Well, I am."

She composedly lifts a glass of water to her lips. "I work with our family's charity organization. I don't need a degree for that."

I nod, noting her snippiness. "Of course. You were always good at philanthropy."

"Getting back to what's important," Jasper says loudly, and reclaiming my attention. "We should cancel the holiday party." And just like that, he's claimed the floor again.

"No way," Bryn says.

"We don't want people learning the status of Father's health."

"Then let's not tell them," Spencer says. "I've invited colleagues and business associates. It's important that I make contact with them." His expression has turned serious. It's the first time I've seen him this way. His all-business demeanor is actually very attractive.

"Plus, we've put a lot of time and attention into this event," Bryn says. "People are flying in from all over the world." She shakes her head. "It's too late to cancel."

Jasper's gaze holds mine captive. "Fine, but no one learns about Father's condition. Got it?"

I narrow my eyes at him. Now it's clear why Bryn sometimes refers to him as Ace. He's sitting high and mighty, calling the shots like he's dealing all the cards. Although he's made my body experience sensations it has never felt before, he's not in charge of me.

"What exactly is your father's condition?" I ask, knowing his blood pressure just spiked.

Jasper looks at Bryn as if to say, "See look what you brought upon this family." Then he looks at Spencer, me, then Bryn again. "Do we agree?"

Ah… He's ignoring me.

"May he burn in hell," Bryn says under her breath and then takes a long drink from her glass of ice water.

Jasper frowns at her then straightens his face so quickly that if I had blinked, I would've missed it.

Note taken.

Let's Not Talk

HOLLY HENDERSON

Plates are empty. Spencer has excused himself from the table. Jasper reminds me that we are to meet in his father's office to go over what's permissible as far as my investigation of the Blackstones. Bryn wants to join us, but he insists that she deals with the logistics of the party.

"Plus, you're too close to Miss Henderson," he says. "I need to be alone with her to set the ground rules. Don't worry. I won't hurt her." He's smirking. I wonder if Bryn susses out what's behind that look in his eyes. Jasper Blackstone wants to bang.

"It's Holly. Not Miss Henderson," Bryn says.

He looks at her with a blank stare. I wonder if he's thinking, "Oh little sister, I've called her Holly and I've made her scream my name too."

Jasper doesn't even glance at me when he says, "I'll see you upstairs Holly. William will escort you to my office." Then he leaves.

Bryn and I stare at each other. I feel exposed and so I squirm in my chair.

"Be careful," she says.

"I will be."

"I warned you."

I nod. "I know—warning heeded."

WARNING NOT HEEDED, I think, standing in front of the big dark-wood door that looks as if it's the entrance to a castle. The office is on a fourth floor that looking at the mansion from the outside, I couldn't see existed. I use a brass knocker, hitting the wood twice to let Jasper know I'm here.

When he opens the door, his sexy eyes are ablaze. He takes me by the wrist, pulls me inside and then presses me against the wall next to the heavy door as it closes slowly. Our gazes are fixed as he bolts three locks.

"What's wrong with your father?" I whisper.

"He's dying," Jasper says and then smashes his hungry lips on mine.

Our tongues tangle, lips caress. His stiff cock grinds against my already sensitive slit. Our kissing and rubbing causes sensations to soar through my sex, making my legs weak.

"Why are you teasing me?" he whispers, although I'm not sure what he's talking about. But the fact that he outright admitted that his father is dying isn't lost on me.

I moan as Jasper's breath, lips, and tongue slide up and down the side of my neck, sending tingling sensations of pleasure to all of my most sensitive spots. "Why does Bryn have so much animosity toward your father?" I ask, trying to keep my head in this game.

Jasper stops abruptly. The look in his eyes isn't anger, and that's a relief.

"Am I boring you, Holly?" he whispers lustfully.

A naughty smile comes across my lips. "No."

One of his eyebrows quirks up as he takes my sweater by the hem and guides it up. I lift my arms as he finishes yanking it over my head and then throwing it on the hardwood floor. But I have on a thin button front shirt under the sweater, worn for an extra layer of warmth. He stares at the garment as if it's an unfortunate barrier.

But then he sees my nipples poking my white

blouse. I grip the back of his head as he bites one and then the other in a very sensual way.

I moan and kiss the top of his head. Then Jasper rips my blouse open. Buttons fly in every direction. Jasper presses his erection against me as he leans back to get an eyeful of my breasts which are contained in a thin black lace bra.

We smirk at each other.

"Get naked," he whispers thickly.

I narrow my eyes sultrily. "You get naked."

Jasper snorts a chuckle. He seems to like my boldness. It feels really powerful to order someone around who's always barking orders at everybody else.

We both take off our clothes as fast as we can.

Now here we stand, staring at each other with nothing on until Jasper grabs my sex, stuffing his fingers deep into my wetness, plunging in and out like a jackhammer.

I grab hold of his muscular shoulders. "Oh that feels so…" I whimper.

Suddenly, he spins me around, guides me to the red velvet sofa, and sets my knees on the cushion, spreading my thighs. "Don't move."

Games… He loves the games.

Suspense grips me as my dazed gaze takes in

dreary daylight and an ice-covered lawn that stops at the edge of a cliff with a gray body of water in the distance. I can feel my wetness dampening the insides of my thighs. I listen to a condom packet rip. I close my eyes, bracing for impact. Then his hot, soft tongue sinks into my asshole, prodding me before sliding down to the bottom of my sex. There's no way he doesn't do this much. He's so sensual. So uninhibited. So experienced. And I am reeling, losing it, squeezing the top of the sofa, close to passing out. I have no idea what's happening to me down below. I can't distinguish between what is a finger and what is a tongue. All I know is that I am being stimulated with precision. My clit is involved. My thighs shiver. The orgasm builds and builds until...

"Ah!" I cry out loud and hard to match the magnitude of the pleasure ripping through me.

The feeling lingers long and when it has had its fill of me, I flop over the top of the sofa like a rag doll.

"Damn, you're so wet," he whispers.

Only because of you, Jasper Blackstone.

He takes me by my hips, I know what comes next. He's earned what comes next.

I gasp as he slams himself inside me, filling me

with his amazing cock. Nothing goes unspent as Jasper thrusts in and out of me. I feel it all. But my body is jolting. His pumping is punishing. He journeys so deep inside of me that it aches but when he pulls out my sex flickers with pleasure.

Then Jasper stops, while he's deep inside me, pushing and pushing. I gasp, gripping the sofa. Loving how deep he's journeyed. He puts his mouth to my ear. "Don't ever ask me questions when I'm ready to fuck you," he whispers.

I'm about to tell him to go to hell, but he starts pounding me again, hard and punishing.

His mouth is near my ear again. "Got it?"

I tighten my walls around his cock, twisting my body to glare at him defiantly. "Do it again."

He takes the bait and it takes four thrusts before he grunts and groans and comes his brains out.

JASPER DOESN'T TAKE HIMSELF OUT OF ME AS HE turns me away from the window to sit on his lap.

"I'm not done with you yet," he announces as his hands knead my breasts. He likes squeezing my nipples. When I tense up against him, he squeezes them some more.

"If that was punishment, then I won," I say with a smirk.

Suddenly, I'm lying on the sofa, and we're kissing as if there were no tomorrow—deep, hot, and sensual. He's touching me everywhere. I grasp at his hard body.

Then we roll effortlessly onto the floor. My desire level is too high. I'm too dizzy.

"Oh, Jasper," I moan.

Saying his name makes him kiss me more passionately. Minutes pass. We can't stop. Then he separates my knees, and then my thighs, and slides a brand new erection into my soaking sex.

I sigh, loving his soft, indulgent strokes. Our lips and tongues make art as he shifts in and out of me. My throat moans without my direction.

Jasper moves in and out, carefully searching for hot-spots. I gasp when he grazes it. *Right there.* He reconnects with that sensitive area and stimulates me until a blindingly pleasurable sensation seizes my sex, causing me to pitch my head back and cry out.

Jasper increases the speed of his pumping. Damn, it feels so good that sensations sparks under my hood yet again. Our eyes stay locked. I don't know what feels better—my sex or my heart. Then he squeezes his eyes shut as he grunts and his body quakes. I cannot look away from the gratification on his face that my body is giving him. He's staring at me too, and neither of us moves a muscle. I could remain beneath him forever. His skin smells so divine. A scent that's all his own is intermingled with mine.

"I smell me on you," I whisper.

"I couldn't wash you off," he admits.

"Me neither."

His eyebrows pull then release. "I can't fall in love with you, Holly."

I open my mouth to ask why not but then press my lips and swallow. "You call me Holly now, so at least we're friends, right?"

He snorts, wearing a weak smile. "You're always working, aren't you?"

I frown confused. "What do you mean, I'm working?"

"This is amazing, what we're doing, but I will protect my family from you, Miss Henderson."

Tension raced through my lips. "Get off of me," I hiss.

He doesn't even hesitate.

Once I'm free of him, I struggle to my feet and rush to put on my pants. But I'm having a hard time getting them on. My eyes are too watery.

"Holly," he whispers.

I stop in the middle of zipping my pants. At least he's back to calling me by my first name. "What?"

"Just gather the rest of your things. I'll show you the way back to your room. No one will see you."

I release a breath that's full of pain. Of course he isn't going to apologize for being a jerk. Of course he isn't going to gather me in his arms and say something that makes me feel as though he will eventually value me as more than his secret lay.

Without another word, I collected my sweater, shirt, and shoes. I'm proud of myself for staving off the tears.

I look at him when I'm ready. There's something in his eyes that looks a lot like regret as he opens a large cabinet door. He then pushes the shelves which hold stacks of books. A landing and a staircase is revealed. *Wow… so many secrets.*

Jasper walks into the space as if he's done it a million times. I on the other hand am amazed by what's happening. I almost think that I dreamt Jasper escaping through the wardrobe in my bedroom. But now I know I didn't dream it. After a brief hesitation, I follow him down a dusky flight of stairs. There are sconces in the wall. We walk down a hallway. The light gives off a gory ambiance that matches the pain I feel inside. Then he pulls open a door, pushes through another, and holds it open for me.

I stop after entering my guest room and look back into the dark secret space. *What kind of house is this?* "Jasper," I say, my eyes pinned to those two high-backed chairs.

"Yes," he whispers. His tone is tender. Maybe he can sense what I'm going to say.

"Don't come visit me again. We're done. Leave."

He stands still for a few beats. But then turns his back on me and disappears into the abyss.

Secrets Mount

HOLLY HENDERSON

Warm water sprays my face from the top of my head. I'm showering, determined to wash Jasper's scent off of me. Having sex with Jasper could get me a lot of answers to questions I have about his family. I mean, I'd gotten him to verify that his father is dying. That's a big reveal. No one knows that about Randolph Blackstone. I could call a few editors I know and score a nice payday with that intel. But I would never do that to him or Bryn. It's clear that I'm playing a harmful game with my heart. Perhaps having sex with Jasper Blackstone is an exercise I should avoid like the plague. Three sexual encounters in less than twenty-four hours is a lot of sex. And I have asked him questions during our time together. I close my eyes and sigh gravely. I can see how he would believe that I'm taking advantage of our intimacy. But isn't he doing the same?

Maybe he isn't.

Maybe I'm the only one who's using sex to my advantage.

"Shit," I whisper, vowing to use other proven methods to acquire enough information to make Bryn happy so I can finish my assignment and get the hell out of the Blackstone mansion.

I put on a pair of jeans, a sweater, and warm boots. I decide to focus more on work and less on Jasper. The first person I want to talk to is Gina. I suspect she's sleeping with two Blackstone brothers. Also, she's very integrated into the family. I want to know why that is and how it happened? Perhaps she's sleeping with Jasper too. She looks as if she's been around the block a number of times. Maybe she's the reason why Jasper is so good at sex. A man doesn't acquire his kind of skills by osmosis. He has to be fucking someone, and doing it a lot.

I ask William if he knows where I can find Gina.

"Ms. Jones is at the pool," he says.

I tilt my head slightly, intrigued. "She's swimming in the cold?"

"It's an indoor pool."

"Oh, I see." I look down at my outfit. I'm over-dressed. "Do you have bathing suits for guests?"

He tells me unused swimsuits are located in the changing room. He offers to escort me to the swimming pool, but I assure him that if he points me in the right direction, then I can find it on my own.

———

The indoor swimming pool is designed in the style of a Roman bathhouse with blue-and-orange decorative Mediterranean tiles covering the bottom and edges. I stand at the edge, watching Gina finish a lap. She's a smooth and graceful swimmer.

When she makes it to the end, she removes her goggles and swipes a hand down her face to remove the extra water. Seeing me appears to take her by surprise.

"What are you doing here?" she asks bitingly.

I dive in the best I can. The warm water engulfs me as I swim to her. I contemplate an approach as my arms strike the water and legs kick. A person in Gina's position is always a hard nut to crack. She's loyal to the Blackstones while being placed at the bottom of their totem pole. She's convinced herself that she's lower than they are. Since I suspect she's already labeled me competition, I'm determined to let her win.

I swim the last few feet underwater. Her legs are against the side of the pool. As I predicted, she stays put.

"Whew," I utter, catching my breath while swiping water off my face. "You're so much better at that than I am. I can tell you've trained professionally."

Gina's eyebrows furrows. I see she's taken aback by my observation. "Yes, I have trained." She shrugs indifferently. "In junior high. That was a long time ago, though." A veil of sadness covers her face, but is quickly replaced by a look of toughness. "What do you want?"

I press my back against the wall as my breathing starts to normalize. I lift my legs to float above water. "I don't want anything. It's cold out and this is a warm swimming pool." I cast a glance at her. "You really are a good swimmer."

"Thank you," she mutters after a few beats. "You're okay too."

"Are you kidding me? What you saw was the best I could ever do." I laugh softly.

She smiles, thankfully. "I was really good when I competed. I never lost a match."

"Why did you quit?"

She frowns then shakes her head as if she's saying no to whatever bad memory that's haunting her. "I just quit."

"Oh," I say, nodding understandingly.

Gina studies me for a moment. "Men are just pigs, aren't they?"

"They can be. You're with Asher. Is he a pig?" I'm digging.

After a moment of silence, she sighs. "No, but Spencer…"

I wait patiently for her to finish.

"He's a flirt," I say to lead her on.

"Don't think you're special to him because you're not." Her tone is biting.

I look into her eyes. So Spencer's the one she's into, not Asher. Maybe she's the reason behind Asher's crossing the line question.

Finally she sighs. "He can be crude."

"Spencer?" I ask frowning.

She stares at the water as if transfixed by it. "He's…"

I wait. I have a feeling she's not going to say

anything else about Spencer so I think of something to keep her talking.

I stare unfocused at the water too. "Someone like that would be crude to all women."

"Someone like what?" she snaps in Spencer's defense.

Good. She took the bait.

I float my legs above the surface, appearing relaxed, even though deep down I'm anxious.

"Someone who doesn't respect other people," I say.

"Everybody doesn't deserve respect. Do you think mass murderers deserve respect?"

Why so angry?

I look at her. Her face is red and expression pinched. "Do you think you deserve respect?"

Gina jerks her head back. She opens her mouth then closes it.

"All human beings are born whole," I say. "Then we have to survive those around us. Right?"

She snorts facetiously. "Or the swim coach."

I shake my head. "Yes, and him too."

We stare at each other for a long moment. I know that saying I'm sorry for the abuse I perceive she had suffered is the wrong thing to say. Silence is my best tool at this moment, along with empathetic eyes which are real. I truly feel for Gina and am quickly beginning to like her.

"I can teach you how to be a better swimmer" —she smiles timidly—"if you like?"

My face lights up. "I absolutely like!"

"Okay. First, let's work on your kick," she says.

———

FOR A WHILE, GINA SHOWS ME HOW TO KICK MY legs. Then we work on my arm strokes and head movements. Once we put them all together, I'm gliding across the water like a pro. I'm amazed at how good she is at teaching. Then I dive into the water from the opposite side of the swimming pool as a final exam, showing her how well I've grasped her lesson.

When I make it to the end of the pool, Gina claps. "You got it! That was perfect."

I lift myself out of the water and hug her. "Well, you were the perfect teacher."

We smile at each other, realizing that our moment of victory has obliterated the wall between us. Then servers bring us drinks and lunch. We sit in the lounge chairs, watching the blue water gently ripple on the surface.

I bite into my avocado and turkey sandwich. "Umm." I close my eyes to relish the flavors. "They serve the best food at this haunted mansion." I laugh softly.

She chuckles. "Bart is an extraordinary chef."

I note that she speaks the chef's name as though she knows him well.

"I would gain fifty pounds in one month if I lived in this place," I say with a laugh. "I would not hold back or watch my diet or anything. I would just eat it all. No shame in my game."

Gina tosses her head back and laughs. "They're just showing off for the guest. Normally, they don't eat so exquisitely. No one eats around here. Bryn is almost as skinny as the skeleton in my high school science classroom."

I laugh at her analogy. Bryn is pretty thin. However, I see an opportunity to lead Gina down a path and find out what she knows about Bryn. "She didn't used to be so thin. I mean, she was always slim, but now…" I raise my eyebrows.

Gina snorts facetiously. "She needs help. And they think I'm screwed up in the head. Ha!"

"I don't think your head is screwed up at all," I say. "I know screwed up in the head and you're not it." Then I tell her the story about my father and how many times he's gone to prison and how my mom had been checked out since the day I was born. "I mean, I think I was born in Northern California, but then we moved to somewhere in Texas, then Washington State. We ended up in Omaha, Nebraska, until I was in the tenth grade, and then we moved to Pittsburgh. That's where my mom got sick and passed away."

Gina's jaw had dropped in the middle of my story, but now her mouth is still caught open. "So you lost your mom?"

I gaze into her watery eyes. I feel a connection. I think we are kindred souls.

"You lost your mom too?" I whisper past my tight throat.

She nods stiffly.

I can't let her sadness and my sadness take me off course, so I peer down at my thighs to push away my pain. "My mom was wounded, very wounded which made her not that great of a mother."

"Neither was mine," Gina says with a sigh. "But I still miss her."

I face her with a tight smile. "Well, Pittsburgh is where my life changed for the best."

Her eyebrows flash up with curiosity. "How so?"

I'm happy she cares to know. "Well, my dad had warrants for his arrest in three states, so he changed our names and used fake report cards to enroll me in school. But I think Principal Carlisle knew my family was a fraud and took pity on me."

"Was your principal a he or a she?"

"He was actually a he," I say.

She seems conflicted by that revelation.

"Like I said, some men are pigs, but the majority are not."

She goes inward again. I recognize that place. It's the dark part of her soul where criticism and shame resides.

"But really, I think you're a great swim teacher," I say to lead her back to the moment.

Gina appears conflicted as she examines my smile. "Thanks, but… You know what I am, right?" She keeps her voice low.

"You're Asher's girlfriend," I say.

Her snort is full of pain and shame. "Not really."

I wait for her to reveal who she is but silence continues to prevail. I back away from leading her deeper into bearing her soul. There's a line I refuse to cross when it comes to gathering information, and exploiting someone's real pain is one of them.

"You know what?" I ask in a more enthusiastic tone. "I know a lot of people. Ever heard of Dan Folks?"

She nods. "Of course I have."

"He runs swim programs for kids all across the country. I can contact him and see if he has a spot for you as an assistant coach. Not pressuring you, but if you choose, I'll make it happen."

She watches me as though she's determining my credibility. "What do you want in return?"

It's time to be honest. "I'm not going to lie. I came out here with an agenda. I'm doing all this research for Bryn's book, and I thought I could learn something from you that the boys won't reveal to me. But I feel like we've connected. You've given me a great afternoon"—I hold up my sandwich—"Bart has given me this, and that's all I need." I take a bite and relish the taste as I chew.

Gina laughs softly. "Well…" Her body seems more relaxed. That's a good sign. "There's not much to the Blackstones other than that they're rich. Some of the men fuck prostitutes. I mean, Jasper doesn't. We tried it once, and that was it."

She's a prostitute?

Does Bryn know?

However, I want to know more about this experience she had with Jasper.

"What do you mean you tried it once with Jasper?" I ask, hiding how jarred I am by her revelation.

"He couldn't get it up."

I work like hell to not expose my surprise on my face. I feel as if there's a lot about their encounter Gina is leaving out, but I won't push.

"Everyone knows he can't keep it up," she says. "That's why he's such a miserable prick. But Spencer—he's one of those guys who has to degrade women to get off. You know, whip, hit, strangle, bite… But it's not his fault. He's…" She presses her lips like she refuses to say more. "Just, I wouldn't go there if I were you. But the father, Randolph, he *is* the devil."

The look in her eyes—she's not exaggerating. "What do you mean?" I'm barely able to squeeze past my tight throat.

I see her mind working behind her eyes, trying to assess if it's safe to say more. After a moment, she checks over her shoulder then inclines her body closer to me. "I'm twenty-three, which makes me too old for that old man."

"Randolph?" I ask.

"Yes. Him."

My eyebrows shoot up. "How old does he like them?"

She holds still for a moment. Her mouth is caught open, her answer, stalled. Suddenly, she rubs her eyes as she groans loudly. "You know what? I can't coach kids. I'm too damaged."

Her agony and all the crap that haunts her washes over me. My expression cradles her empathetically. "No, you're not, Gina. You're a survivor. And this moment is all that matters, and the next and the next. Got it?" I watch her intensely. I want her to know how much I meant what I said.

She nods mildly.

"And I would never take back my offer to contact Coach Dan on your behalf," I say. "Absolutely never."

Gina smiles pensively then looks down to scratch her thigh. I wonder what she's thinking. I'm about to ask when she says, "They are hiding lots of secrets, though." She searches past me then looks over her shoulder. "I think it has something to do with Amelia. I don't think she and Randolph were ever married."

I swallow the urge to gasp and maintain my composure. "Why not?"

She swings her legs around to sit on the edge of the lounge chair, facing me. "Randolph's like a rich guy who spends all his time feeding his depraved habits. Jasper's the one who keeps the money flowing. But I don't think Jasper knows his father like he thinks he does."

"Well, what doesn't he know?" I ask, keeping my excitement under wraps.

She checks over both shoulders again and then brings her mouth close to my ear and whispers, "I can't tell you. But it's bad, very bad."

I put my mouth to her ear. "How bad is it?"

She leans back and shakes her head. "I've already said too much."

Silence falls between us for a moment, but since I have her talking, my curiosity wants to be fed some more. So, I ask Gina where's she from and more about her parents. Our stories aren't that dissimilar. She's from a trailer park in Chattanooga, Tennessee. Her mother would go from one man to another, all of whom would abuse the both of them. Then one day, she escaped her hellhole when she started working for an online call-girl service. Randolph Blackstone solicited her services when he came to town on business.

"He kept me around longer than he normally

keeps girls because I reminded him of his favorite actress."

"Marilyn Monroe," I say.

"Bingo," she replies. "Then one day, he couldn't get it up for me anymore, so I started servicing his business associates instead." Her tone is so frank. I have to remind myself that we are talking about the illegal business of prostitution.

"And what about his sons?" I quickly throw in, hoping she'll answer.

Silence falls again.

Then she shakes her head. "No. They're not business. They're my…"

I wait.

Again, she says nothing.

I grunt thoughtfully as she squirms uncomfortably on top of her chair. I must keep her talking.

"Randolph   Blackstone   in   Chattanooga, Tennessee. I wonder what he was doing there," I muse.

Gina rises to her feet and stands over me.

I look up at her gorgeous figure and pretty face.

"He stayed at my apartment a lot, but on most occasions…" Then she whispers an address in my ear before strolling off.

I take note of that address in my head.

I sit at the pool for a while to think. Holy shit, I think I'm on the precipice of something really big. I've been in these shoes before in the case of the Howsleys. All it had taken was one radical element to give me the key I needed to unlock their vault of secrets. I believe Gina just handed me that key. Jasper will be watching me like a hawk, though. I can't just leave in the middle of my visit, and go to Chattanooga. I need to ask someone I could trust to do it for me. I know just who to call.

Surprise Surprise

HOLLY HENDERSON

O n the walk back to the mansion, I call my colleague Kylie Neeland.

The line rings twice before she says, "Hello?"

"Hi Kylie, it's me, Holly Henderson."

She sneezes. "I know. Your name came up on my screen. That's why I answered. I figured if the great Holly Henderson is calling me, then I'm interested to know why. So what's going on?" She sounds stuffy but eager to hear what I have to say.

It's chillier out now that my hair is damp but pulled in a bun. I hug myself as I walk slowly away from the house and down a secluded path flanked by tall evergreens for more privacy. "I'm at the Blackstone Family mansion."

"Oh, the evil Vlads. Wait, they invited *you* to the party? They must have a death wish."

I snort a chuckle. "I'm actually spending Christmas with them."

"Get out of here." I can't see her, but I can tell she pepped up quite a bit after hearing that.

"Yes. Long story short, Bryn hired me to do some deep investigation of her family. She's writing the family's biography."

Kylie scoffs. "I doubt it'll tell the whole truth."

"You never know," I say, as I stop and stand against a tall tree to shield myself from an icy breeze that's blowing through this path I found.

"Oh, I know," she strongly claims. "And is Jasper okay with her little book?"

I roll my eyes, thinking about how much Jasper isn't with the program. "Not, really."

"I didn't think he would be," she says, sounding less sick than she had when we first started our conversation. "There's a reason no one else has picked up where I left off. Actually, you're the first person who's called to inquire about what I may have found out about them. I presume that's why you're calling."

I try not to hesitate for too long. No, I didn't call to learn what she discovered about the Blackstones but I sure will like to know. "You presume right," I say. "Would you care to share?"

"I can't."

I jerk my head back in surprise. "Why not?"

"I'm not allowed to say."

"Is it because of Jasper?"

"I'm not allowed to say."

That would be a yes. "Did it have anything to do with what happened at the coroner's office?"

She pauses. "I'm not allowed to say."

That's another yes. "Did your investigation of the family ever take you to Chattanooga?"

"Chattanooga? What's in Chattanooga?"

That was a no.

"And by the way, if you're in their house, asking me these questions, then I'm going to hang up."

I bend and expand my freezing fingers, trying to keep the blood flowing. "I'm not in the house. But, I can't leave and I have an address in Chattanooga. Care to check out things for me?"

KYLIE SAID SHE WOULD LOAD UP ON VITAMIN C AND Tylenol and take the first flight from New York City to Chattanooga, Tennessee. I can't wait to hear what she finds. Meanwhile, I hightail it back to the main house to defrost. A lot of activity is going on as catering and delivery vans line up along the driveway. This might be my opportunity to evade William. Instead of entering through the main back doors, I walk around to the side of the house to check and see if the door near Bryn's room is open. It is.

I sigh indulgently after entering the perfectly warm house. Despite so many people being here this afternoon, I can't hear a thing. The sound proofing here is great despite this being a very old manor.

However, I'm inside the Blackstone mansion, William is nowhere in sight, and I have a lot of questions about Randolph Blackstone. I wish there was a staircase on this side of this house. Usually in a mansion like this there's more than a few. Maybe Bryn can help.

I rap lightly on her bedroom door, trying to keep my knock quiet. I don't want William to hear my knock echoing in the hallway.

I wait. I ball my fist to knock again, but something tells me to turn the knob and so I do it. I slowly open the door and then gasp with surprise. The space isn't a bedroom. It's a staircase.

Grimacing, I turn toward the direction where I imagine William is standing and waiting for me. Why would he purposely mislead me? And I can't call him out on it because then he'll report back to Jasper. They both will know that I've gone snooping. Regardless, I carefully, softly close the door behind me and then pad up the staircase. Randolph's bedroom is on the third floor. It would be great to get a look at him, confirm that he is indeed in a bad way. Maybe I'll snap a photo of him with my cell-phone if I'm lucky enough to get that close to him.

I make it to the third level and inch by inch, open the door. I hold my breath and stand very still as I watch the backside of Jasper as he speaks to a man in a suit. I can't hear what they're saying but a woman wearing a floral shirt, the kind nurses wear, and black pants steps out into the hallway to join them.

Jasper's physique is so yummy. For a moment I recall him on top of me, inside me. I can't believe I ended things between us. I'll have to figure out a way to let him know I've changed my mind about wanting him to stay away from me. I don't want that, not anymore.

I stifle a gasp as the man in the suit turns in my direction. Oh no… Jasper is twisting his body. Soon he'll be looking at the door too. My heart is beating a mile a minute as I carefully creep the door closed. I'm padding down the stairs but instead of going back to the first floor, I exit onto the second level. This hallway is quiet.

Down the corridor I walk, turning knobs to locked doors until I turn into a vast library. I'm thinking it's a permissible space so I enter and let my gaze roam the room, books are placed on built-in shelves that go all the way up to the ceiling. I wonder what a man like Randolph Blackstone reads. Or maybe he doesn't read. Maybe the books are stacked for the purpose of making the room look like a library.

I slide my finger across lime green cloth spines of old books which have titles written in gold letters. Many are classics. Then, I stop at a title that piques my interest. *Slave* by Ancient Rome. That's odd. I never knew Ancient Rome was an author.

"How are you this afternoon?"

I jump startled and then turn to see Jasper standing behind me. He's close. I wonder how long he's been standing there.

"Hi," I say breathlessly, pressing a hand over my pounding heart.

His gaze sucks me into his vortex. "What are you doing?"

My lips part. I can't figure out what to say right away. I swallow to reset my brain, and then say, "Enjoying the library." I slide the book that caught my attention off the shelf. "Slave?" I read and look to him for comment.

Jasper closes the distance between us. I can't move a muscle as he stands right in front of me. With each breath his chest rises high and falls low smoothly, and so does mine.

"Did you enjoy your swim?" he asks in a low voice as he carefully takes the book out of my hand.

My lips have a mind of their own. They incline themselves toward his mouth. It feels as if we should be kissing already.

"I did," I barely say. Then, I swallow. "Can I ask you something?"

He cracks a smirk. "Could I stop you?"

I snort softly and he gently closes his eyes as my breath flutters across his face.

"No," I say in a tight voice.

He's waiting for me to speak.

"Why does Bryn whisper all the time?" My eyes veer up and points to two corners of the room. "Are you watching us? Are spy cameras installed throughout this house?"

"If there were spy cameras through the house, I would be watching you every second of the day, Holly. But no. Not anymore."

My lips part. I don't know which part of his response to respond to first. "Not anymore?"

"No. We grew up with cameras in the house but I had them removed."

My eyebrows quirk up with intrigue. "After your father fell ill?"

"Yes."

It's such a turn on when he answers a direct question with a quick and direct answer. I'm creaming for him.

"So, Holly." His whisper savors of lust. "The last thing you said to me—do you still you mean it? I want to be with you tonight."

My heart pounds so hard that I can feel the vibrations in my throat. No, not anymore, I want to say in a mad rush of words. "It depends," I say instead.

"On what?"

I grasp the book in his hand and attempt to reclaim it. But Jasper has a tight grip on it. He's not giving it back.

"What are you hiding?"

His smirk turns sexier. "It's not my job to tell you what I'm hiding. It's your job to figure it out."

I shake my head even though I love his answer. It contains a dare and I'm more than ready to rise to the challenge. "Is that all you want from me Jasper Blackstone is to fuck me?"

His fingers trail softly down the side of my face as he maintains steady eye contact. "I love fucking you?"

Sensations flutter in my chest. The heat emanating from him is dizzying. I want to kiss him already. I want to touch him, feel to see if he's hard.

My breaths are craggy but still, I play it cool. "So you don't want to get to know me?"

"I know everything about you."

I toss my head into a side tilt. "You do?"

With a straight face he tells me my father's name is Harper Henderson and then does a rundown of my dad's petty criminal record with detailed precision. He says my mom's name was Gayle Henderson, he pauses before saying, "And she's deceased. I'm sorry."

He actually said that with empathy.

"I'm not surprised you've performed a check on me," I say.

"I know that you're not surprised."

I fold my arms, gazing into his clear eyes. "Am I your enemy? Is that why you're checking on me and keeping me close?"

Very slightly, he shakes his head. "I call you Holly, don't I?"

We should kiss now.

"Yes," I reply breathlessly. I audibly clear my throat to rid the lust out of what I'm going to say next. "Then we're friends?"

His arms moves as though he wants to touch me but then changes his mind. "We're beyond friends, Holly. I want you to be…"

"Excuse me, Jasper," a man says.

Jasper coolly turns toward the entrance to the library. I should look to see who has joined us too but I can't take my eyes off Jasper's perfect profile. What a gorgeous man he is. He's graced with a sort of classic kind of beauty—manly, sensual, and timeless. I've seen photos of Randolph Blackstone and the two do not favor one another very much. I wonder what Amelia looked like. I bet he resembles her.

"You're needed upstairs," the man says.

Finally, I force myself to look away from Jasper

and at a man who's wearing a suit similar to the one William wears.

"Thank you, Nigel," Jasper replies.

Nigel bows his head and walks away, leaving us alone again.

"Is your father okay?" I ask him.

"No," he answers without pause, which makes my sex tremble for him. Then he nods sharply. "Later, Holly."

Every cell in my body reaches for him. "Later, Jasper." I'm barely audible.

For a moment his gaze seems to sink into my face and then retract. He turns away from me. His confident gait commands my full attention until he's out of sight. My legs grow weak urging me to find the nearest piece of furniture to sit down on. I plop down on a sturdy velvety gray sofa.

What am I going to do when December 26th comes and I'm back on the road heading home? Giving up Jasper will be like all of a sudden having to stop eating my favorite ice cream. Then, the empty space where the book I took off the shelf catches my eye. He took the book with him.

"Hmm…"

That's odd.

I GO BACK TO MY ROOM AND SPEND A LONG TIME ON my laptop. First, I write everything I can remember from my conversation with Gina at the pool. I write what I saw in the third floor hallway, and mention William's misleading me. I record other odd details like the exchange between Asher and Spencer at the table and the secret corridor that Jasper escorted me through. I was too distraught to really pay attention to what was around me but I could feel the draftiness and emptiness. I suspect that there are networks of hallways which run throughout this huge manor.

William had informed me upon returning to my room that dinner would be served in my quarters tonight due to kitchen staff and house staff preparing for tomorrow's party. I tried to call Bryn several times but my calls went straight to voicemail. I wonder if she's even on the premises. Are any of the Blackstone siblings in the house? Jasper is definitely staying in the cottage. Gina said that Randolph was or is the devil. I wonder… are the memories too awful in this house for them to spend much time inside it?

Dinner is still served in three courses along with

a bottle of Merlot. The first course is an English garden beet root salad. The main course is traditional duck breast confit with creamy wild mushroom risotto. And the third course is the most delicious sticky toffee pudding I've ever eaten.

By dinner's end, I've drunk nearly the entire bottle of wine. I shower, dry my hair, moisturize with my sweet vanilla body cream and crawl into bed. Jasper said he'll visit me tonight. I yawn as I check the time on my cellphone. It's 10:08 p.m. I wonder if he'll still come see me.

Maybe not.

But I hope so.

Amelia's Old Friend

HOLLY HENDERSON

DECEMBER 23

"Holly," he calls in the dark. His voice is tender, masculine, sensual.

I'm drowsy but I know it's him—Jasper Blackstone.

No lights. The mood is set. I'm naked and so is he. His skin is warm, body hard. He's on top of me. I'm experiencing euphoria tasting his mouth.

My sigh trembles as he moves into me, filling me.

We're kissing.

My desire climbs and climbs—I am high.

My sex is piqued.

I arch my back.

My nipples are moistened, stimulated. *Umm this feels so delicious.* I wince and stiffen upon his gentle bite, he warns me that he's going to come.

He wants me too much, he says.

He's addicted to me.

I'm so beautiful.

So soft, he says too.

Everything he loves in a woman.

"Come, baby."

He pumps diligently. And we've done this enough for me to know exactly what to do.

I raise my hips toward the intensity.

I feel it.

I feel it more.

More…

"Oh," I whimper as an orgasm streaks through my hood.

Then he grunts, curses, and shivers on top of me.

Jasper draws me against his naked body. He's all muscle and delicious sandalwood, apple, and black pepper scented cologne worn mild by the day.

I'm enraptured.

6:00 A.M.

My alarm rings and I wake up quickly. I feel for Jasper beside me. He is gone. Disappointed, I roll back onto my pillow and close my eyes.

He was definitely with me last night. I can smell him on my sheets and on my skin. I can feel him too. His touch is like a shadow spreading over me. After we made love, he was so tender with me, stroking my body until I fell asleep.

He whispered something.

What did he say?

I can't remember.

My cellphone beeps that I have a text message.

8:00 A.M.

I mindfully ate peach crepes with fluffy scrambled eggs for breakfast. Although I was in a rush, I didn't want to rush. Not through a meal—they're too delicious to rush.

The message I received earlier was from Kylie. She asked me to call her once I was outside of the manor. She must know that Randolph Blackstone kept his home wired to listen to all the activity going on within the walls. I believed Jasper when he said that the system is no longer in use. I'm not sure if he's playing me or not, but my instincts say that he's telling the truth.

Today, I'm following up on the subtle lead given to me by Crystal Preacher. Her mother is Sally Preacher, Amelia's former personal maid and friend. There is more activity at the manor today than there was yesterday. William wasn't even posted outside my door when I walked out of the room. All sorts of delicious scents rise through the house. Some of the aromas are food and others are pine, cinnamon and vanilla, basically Christmas scents.

It's colder than a penguin's bottom this morning. However, I have on a thick turtleneck sweater with a long-sleeve T-shirt, spandex pants under my jeans, two pairs of socks, my fur-lined winter booties and a hefty winter-coat. I keep my head down and avoid as many people as I can on my way to my car. When I make it to the garage it's locked.

"Damn it," I curse under my breath.

It isn't a mystery who did this. To make sure I'm not falsely blaming Jasper for making sure I'm unable to access my car, I press the button to open the center garage door, and it rolls up.

I sigh. "Oh Jasper Blackstone. How naughty art thou."

I can't maneuver my car out of the garage because a wall separates the locked and unlocked area. I stay levelheaded and figure out what to do next. I pull my coat tighter over my chest as I eye the line of catering trucks parked alongside the driveway. Snow flurries start to blow down from the sky and the gray sky adds a greater chill to the cold. But I can't give up now. I must talk to Sally Preacher today.

My first mission is to escape the property without being seen. I walk behind the garage then past a private forest of winter-bare trees. I remain among the sticks as I move toward the perimeter of the property. My fingers are turning to ice, and I'm questioning my sanity when I finally catch sight of a snow covered road.

I didn't have to trudge far before meeting the plowed pavement. *Home free.* I take my cellphone out of my briefcase, and even though my fingers are nearly numb, I perform a regional search for Sally Preacher. Since I'm a pro at searching the white pages, it doesn't take long to locate a Sally Preacher who has a relative named Crystal Preacher. Sally lives in Providence and I have her address. Finally, I can call an Uber.

———

Fifteen minutes later, the car arrives. While I waited I looked for more photos of Amelia Blackstone. I couldn't find any so I texted Kylie and asked if she had one or two.

She messaged back immediately: *Are you using their internet?*

I replied quickly: *No. I'm off the property. My hotspot. Send pics if you have them and I'll call u when I'm in the Uber.*

Kylie answered by sending a gallery of photographs of Amelia Blackstone.

Thawing in the back seat of an Uber I study each photo, enlarging them, taking in every aspect of her face. Then I notice something about Amelia that I wonder if Kylie has ever questioned.

———

"It's one reason why I wanted that coroner's report," Kylie says. "Amelia always looked stressed which made her appear older, but her true age is a mystery."

"But it's in her eyes," I say.

"Yes," Kylie replies. "She's very young to be married to such an old fart."

I hear a flight number being called in the background. "Are you at the airport?"

Kylie coughs then sneezes. "I'm getting ready to board my flight to Chattanooga."

"It's an early flight."

"Well, I'm motivated. And by the way, I'm not supposed to engage in any investigation of that family we talked about. But…"

I smile from ear to ear. "They're your unfinished business."

Silence falls between us.

However, the driver says, "No way," gossiping with whomever she's speaking to through her ear pods.

"Oh, before I board, I want to send you some other facts I've unearthed," Kylie says. "I was supposed to destroy everything I had on them, but I didn't. Maybe you can do something with it."

My email chimes, alerting me of a new message. "Got it. Thanks."

I hear that she's walking fast by her accelerated

breaths. "I'll tell you what I find. Wish us luck?" She ends the call.

The driver, who appears to be barely out of high school, whips around a corner, heading onto the interstate at around fifty miles per hour while laughing.

I figure the best thing for me to do is to keep my head down and pray I make it to Sally Preacher's house in one piece. To distract myself, I open the email Kylie had sent me and start reading. The first attachment is an interview with a college friend of Asher's named Peter Turgot. He claimed people had wanted to get to know Asher because of his abilities as a chemist. Turgot accused Asher of making drugs and said that Bryn's twin had been known around campus as Santa Claus because he would always show up with the best poppers.

However, Kylie notes that she couldn't get anyone on the record about how one of his concoctions ended up causing multiple overdoses. She also sent me a list of people whose palms had allegedly been greased by Jasper. A guy named Benjamin Dow had actually pled guilty to making the drugs. According to Kylie's notes, he was released from prison after serving nine months of an eight-year sentence. She also included a list of her current observations on Benjamin Dow:

Benji's house, San Francisco, CA – $3,789,999

Car – Mercedes G-Wagon

Job – N/A

Bank Account: $16,000,000 + Various annuities and IRAs that cannot be traced back to the Blackstones.

Conclusion: They're paying him off for taking the fall.

My mouth falls open. "Wow," I whisper.

"I'm sorry," the driver says as if she's been waiting for me to speak. "I'll slow my speed."

"Thank you," I reply, even though I wasn't talking to her. Immediately, I feel the car slow and relax a bit.

"So, do you live in that big house?" she asks.

Damn, she wants to talk. "I'm sorry, what's your name again?"

"I'm Tiffany."

"Tiffany, I'm in town visiting friends, but I have an errand to run and—"

"Don't the Blackstones live next door to where I picked you up?"

I close my laptop, giving her my undivided attention. "Yeah, they do," I say leadingly.

"Are they your neighbors?"

"No. I'm just in town visiting a college friend for the holiday."

"Oh. Because there's a weird vibe I get from the Blackstone manor."

I bring exaggerated intrigue to my expression. "Ooh, why's that?"

The car accelerates again. Tiffany has a heavy foot. "They don't really call for Ubers because they're richer than God, but once I picked up this girl. I actually picked her up at the same spot where I picked you up."

"Oh, crazy," I say.

"Yeah. And she was really young, much younger than I am. She had two swollen black eyes and a busted lip. I asked her if anyone hit her, and she said, 'What do you think?' With an attitude and everything. She was really tough, like from-the-streets kind of tough."

"Oh. Then how did you know she was at the Blackstones'?"

She takes a sharp left turn to beat the traffic light, and I hold on to the passenger's side seat to keep from hitting the door.

"Because when we passed by their mansion, she scooted all the way down so no one could see her and kept yelling at me to go faster. It was weird."

"Wow. That is strange. So you think she was roughed up by someone at the Blackstone mansion?"

"I do. Another time, I picked up the brother with the strange eyes. I was just trying to be nice, make conversation, you know. So I said it was strange he called us when they have a lot of cars and more money than God. He told me to just shut up and drive." She shakes her head. "So rude..."

That sounds like Jasper to me. "Yes, I heard one of the brothers is extremely rude." I fight the urge to laugh.

Tiffany watches me through the rearview mirror, and I smile at her.

"So where are you from?" she asks.

I take her change of subject to mean she's done talking about the Blackstones and wants to engage me in more conversation. Since I love hearing people's stories, I tell her that my parents moved a lot and that I was the happiest when we moved to Pittsburgh. Then I ask her where she's from. Tiffany tells me that her parents believe she's in school full-time at Rhode Island Art Institute, but she's taken the year off and used the tuition to travel to Costa Rica and Morocco. She has no idea what she wants to do with her life other than travel.

"Why not start a travel blog?" I ask just as we stop in front of a Dutch-style home with two bare trees on both sides of the yard.

"Nah. I'd rather not do all of that writing."

I nod as I take in the red, green, and white fairy lights strung along the edge of the roof and the inflated Santa Claus and reindeer-drawn sleigh on the lawn. "I get it. Writing isn't for everyone." I open the door and look over my shoulder at Tiffany. "And you're going to wait for me, right?"

"Absolutely," she sings as though she doesn't have a care in the world.

I smile thankfully and exit the back seat.

The sidewalk is shoveled, and since the day is dark, the porch light is on. I stand up straight and make sure my expression looks confident but friendly as I ring the doorbell. I breathe steadily, controlling my nervousness as I wait.

Soon, a plump woman who seems to be wearing a permanent frown opens the door. "Can I help you?" she asks sharply.

The trick to not getting the door slammed in my face is to say all the right things first. "My name is

Holly Henderson, and I'm a guest at the Blackstone manor. Your daughter, Crystal, told me about you."

Her frown turns more severe, and she looks as if she wants to club me to death. However, she doesn't slam the door in my face, and that's a good sign.

"I'm a friend of Bryn's," I say. "She's the reason I'm here."

"She's the reason you're at my door?"

"Sort of, yes."

"Sort of? Explain sort of."

"You worked as a maid for the Blackstones for a number of years."

Sally doesn't say anything. Geez, her personality is not as warm as the Christmas decorations around her house. But I've dealt with hundreds of Sallys during the course of my career.

"Was that a question?" she asks.

"A statement. Listen, for some reason, Bryn hired me to uncover what she needs for a book about her family. Perhaps she wants them to atone for their sins. She and I were college roommates for a year."

Finally, Sally steps out onto the porch and closes the door behind her. She hugs herself to keep warm, even though she's wearing a thick green turtleneck sweater.

"What do you want?" she whispers.

I have to make my question good. I must confirm all my earlier leads. "How old was Amelia Blackstone?"

Sally searches up and down the street, then her eyes fell on Tiffany in the car.

"She's my Uber driver," I explain.

Sally closes the space between us. "I'm forty-seven. Amelia and I were close. Probably best friends, as much as she knew how to have a best friend. But we were the same age." Then her eyes narrow to slits. "That's all I can say."

I feel my incredulous expression. "But that would mean she was fourteen when she had Jasper."

"Was that a question?" she asks.

"Yes."

She studies me for a moment. It's as if she's assessing whether she can trust me or not. "Don't go anywhere." Sally walks into her house and closes the door behind her. A chill runs through me and I shiver. Thankfully, she's back soon and hands me a hairbrush. "This used to be Amelia's."

I frown. "It's a brush."

"Like I said, it used to be Amelia's. Her hair is

still tangled in the bristles." She's sending me a message through her intense stare.

No words are needed. I catch her drift.

"Thank you for this," I say.

Her face is red. "You were never here. You understand?"

I nod resolutely. "No one knows I'm here, and no one will ever know I've been here."

She points her chin at Tiffany. "She knows you're here."

I quickly glance over my shoulder. Tiffany's on the phone again. "I covered my tracks. Believe me. I'm an investigative reporter."

"I know who you are."

My eyebrows quirk up. "You do?"

"Yes. And that Randolph Blackstone is a lecherous bastard. Amelia Rainier had a lot of pain. Make him pay for what he had done to her. That's all I have to say." Sally turns her back on me, walks into her house, and carefully closes the door.

I stand there for a moment and then slip the brush into my purse. I can't take it back to the mansion, I don't want to risk it. So I stop in the middle of the walkway, take out my phone, and call the lab tech I always use to process this sort of sensitive evidence.

Rich, the lab tech, reminds me of the rules before he agrees to accept my delivery. The results cannot be used in a court of law unless the sample is resubmitted by a law enforcement agency. Also, the sample cannot be part of an active law enforcement investigation. I assure him my sample qualifies.

"Then send it on, although we won't have results until after Christmas."

"That's fine," I say and continue walking. "Will tomorrow be too late to send samples to compare with the one I'm sending you today?"

"Nope," he says.

I put my hand on the car door handle. "Great. I'll overnight what I have today."

"I'll be waiting."

Keeping Secrets

HOLLY HENDERSON

Finally, we arrive at the neighbor's gate, where I thank Tiffany for driving me to Sally Preacher's house and then the UPS store where I express mailed the hairbrush to Rich. I practically run the same path to the main house that I took to make it off the property. My pace is so brisk that when I make it to my room, I'm sweating like crazy.

I open the closet and then my suitcase, searching through my dirty clothes for the shirt I wore yesterday when Jasper bit and sucked my nipples through the material. Fourteen years old when she had her first child? I think not. I bet Jasper isn't Amelia's son. I'm sure he left behind enough DNA for testing. However, I need Spencer and Bryn's DNA too. Thank goodness I can pass on Asher's, being that he and Bryn are twins. She will easily cough up a sample for me, but Spencer will be tough.

As I carry my blouse out of the closet, I try to figure out the easiest way of acquiring Spencer's DNA. A face comes to mind, and I turn toward the wall that separates my room from the one next door. Maybe Gina can help. Although I'm not even sure she's in there. I haven't heard a peep from that room as of yet.

"Where have you been?" Jasper asks.

I yelp loudly and jump, pressing my hand over my pounding heart. Jasper's standing in the same spot I found him in when I accidentally walked into this room. He's looking out the window. For a moment, I pause to notice how sexy he looks in black silk twill pants and a crisp white shirt.

"What are you doing in here?" I finally ask.

"I asked, 'Where have you been'?" he insists.

He's being a jerk, which helps me relax a little. I'm no longer intimidated by Asshole-Jasper. "I know what you asked, but you're in my space. I'm not in yours. So, why are you here?"

Finally, he turns to face me. "I'm looking for you."

I feel trapped by his gaze for more reasons than one. First, I have the shirt with his saliva on it in my hands, and I hope he won't ask me what I'm doing with it. Second, I was just about to go to Gina's room to ask if there's any way she can help me collect Spencer's DNA. Basically, Jasper caught me with my hand in the cookie jar.

My head turns dizzy as he approaches me. "Now. Where have you been, Holly?" Jasper takes me by the waist and draws me against his hard body.

"Out taking in the sights."

He narrows an eye suspiciously. "In your car?"

Snarling, I roll my eyes. "No, because you locked my car in your garage." *His cock is hard.*

"No, I didn't," he whispers passionately.

"Yes, you did."

Suddenly, his lips are on mine. Our kissing is always so damn sensual. We have natural chemistry. Our tongues brush each other's delicately, and our lips rub as though they are engaged in an erotic massage. Jasper gently bites my bottom lip and sucks it into his balmy mouth. *What an erotic sensation.* When he releases my lip, I do the same to him, and that drives him mad with lust.

The next thing I know, Jasper guides me to the

bed. I toss the shirt in my hand over my head. *Screw the DNA sample, at least for the moment.* He lifts my leg and pulls off one of my boots and then the other. I try to beat him to the button of my jeans, but he's too fast.

Jasper unbuttons and then yanks them off. "Spread your legs," he whispers thickly.

His eyes are ablaze as I separate my knees. I can feel his gaze stroking the wet crotch of my black lace panties. Fueled by lust, I wonder what he's planning to do next. Jasper drops to his knees, pulls my sex against his face, and begins eating me out through my panties.

Oh my…

I grab two handfuls of bedding as I sigh and squirm until the vigorous and marvelous sensation of orgasm spreads through my sex. My head is woozy with desire as I sit up and reach out to unbutton his expensive pants. He's next.

Jasper's hand seizes my wrist. "Not now," he whispers, even though I can see that he's about to burst. "I want to smell you on my face." He cracks a sexy smirk as he helps me to my feet. He's still rock hard. "What's going on between us stays between us," he warns.

Once again, I feel relegated to being his temporary concubine. But this time I make myself not care. In one statement, he's reminded me of what's really important. Now he's given me even more DNA to send to the lab—his saliva on my panties. *I win.*

"Don't worry," I say bitingly. "My expectations of there being an 'us' are nonexistent."

His eyebrows furrow as if what I said hurt him somehow. But he's the one who started our push-pull relationship.

I walk to the closet, to quickly take off my sweater and put on a fluffy robe. "I mean we don't do much but have sex. I don't know who you are, not for real. And you certainly don't know who I am."

"I know who you are," he claims.

I walk back out to the main room and stand in front of him. "All you know are details about my past. But you don't know me."

There's a glint of a dare in his eyes. Then he checks the face of his expensive wristwatch. "I'm late for my own party."

"Then you better go," I say with manufactured indifference.

Jasper steps closer. Our faces are so close that his escaped breath warms my lips. Then he kisses me sensually, making my head spin all the way to Venus. I'm still somewhere in the clouds when he let's go of me and turns to walk away.

"Jasper," I say breathlessly.

The fire is still in his eyes when he turns to face me.

"I want to have free access to my car," I whisper.

"Who's stopping you from gaining access to your car?"

I smirk. "We're going to do this again?"

He smirks as he scratches his temple. "I'll handle it," he says and then strolls out of my room. Gosh, he's so mesmerizing.

Now that he's gone, I rush to the bathroom and pull the trash bag out of the golden wastebasket. Just as I suspected, there are fresh bags at the bottom. I take three bags and put my panties drenched with Jasper's saliva and my juices in one bag along with the shirt. That leaves two more bags for Spencer and Bryn's DNA samples.

I GO TO GINA'S ROOM AND KNOCK AND KNOCK AND then knock again. I sigh, frustrated. I still wonder if she's ever stayed in that room at all. But why would Bryn lie? And where in the hell is Bryn anyway?

"Hello, Miss Henderson. Is there anything I can get for you?"

I jump startled. It's William, his expression humdrum as usual. I eye him intently. What I ask next may definitely get back to Jasper. But that's fine with me. At this point it's important to learn how Jasper will respond to the moves I make.

"Have you seen Gina?" I ask.

"She is no longer a guest."

I hide my surprise. Why would she leave before the big party? That's odd. "When did she leave?"

"This afternoon."

Damn. I keep how shattered I feel on the inside under wraps. Gina being gone may put a pin in my plans to collect Spencer's DNA. Even though I've been told she's Asher's guest, deep down I get the feeling she's here for Spencer too.

I thank William and assure him that I will not be needing his special services tonight. I'll find my own way to the party.

He bows his head. "Whatever you like." And then, in a rare display of showing some sort of expression on his face, William raises an eyebrow and says, "Also, a garage door opener will be placed on your nightstand during turn-down service."

I thank him, knowing Jasper arranged that little deal. He's also the one who made it impossible for me to drive off the property in my car.

After one more bow, William walks down the hallway. I watch him until he's out of sight. Gnawing on my bottom lip, I'm forced to think about what to do next—and then it comes to me, Plan B.

———

FIGURING IT WILL BE COLD IN THE DARK HALLWAYS, I put on my long coat and grab my cell phone to use the flashlight app to illuminate my path. My stomach flutters as I enter the Blackstone mansion's secret domain through the wardrobe cabinet in my room.

After passing through a hollowed out room lit by one dim light in the ceiling, I enter a dark and drafty corridor where the flooring is concrete. I'm immediately seized by a thick but invisible energy. Whatever that thing is squeezes my body, my brain, and even my soul. It's as if I've entered another universe, one where evil seeks to vanquish good.

There are shallow foyers which lead to doors. Each entryway to a room looks the same. I turn and glare back at the distance I've traveled. This is not the same hallway Jasper brought me through, the one that led out of his office and down a staircase. I somehow missed a turn. Now that I think about it, there could have been another hidden door within that cubicle I entered when I first left Amelia's bedroom. Where I stand now is another aspect of the hidden world within the manor.

I count the number of doors I've already passed, which amount to two, and dig in my coat pockets. I find a business card from a story I had worked on many months ago. I hurry back to the door that leads to Amelia's bedroom and drop the business card in the foyer. There—now I can easily find my way back to where I started.

I try to open a door that appears to lead to the room next to mine but it's locked. I go to the next door. That one is open and I end up in a parlor, which has two scarlet leather sofas with a lacquered coffee table between them. The room smells faintly of cigars. There's no more to this space than that, so I quickly return to the dreary hallway.

I take a right turn. Something feels very odd. I go back to the end of the hallway I just left and use my cellphone flashlight to illuminate my way. Yes. The floor inclines from my room. I think I could be on the third floor or somewhere in between. But there are more doors along the inner part of the house, which means they more than likely are entrances to rooms with no windows. The thought of dark rooms connecting to this ghostly hallway makes me shiver.

My insides are chilled. I've never been one to give into fear but for some reason I am scared. I fight the urge to give up on this seek and find mission. And really… what am I looking for anyway? I don't even know. However, I keep going.

I push my ear against the first door. I hear nothing, not even the faint noise of open space. Slowly, carefully, I turn the handle and then enter a tight dark space.

And now, I hear something.

A woman moans as if she's caught in the throes of good sex. Something tight and irrational grips me. Is it him? Jasper? Is he fucking another woman?

I press both palms on the door and listen harder.

"I love you," a man says, grunting. He's definitely coming.

"I love you too," the woman says tightly.

Gasping softly, I stand straight. That's Bryn. *What the hell?*

Who is she with? She said she wasn't seeing anyone.

"Damn you, Bryn," I mutter before shifting back into the hallway. Apparently, she's lying to me too.

I go in and out of doors, listening for activity. I'm at the last room before turning down another hallway when I hear two men talking. Their voices are muffled a bit but I can still make out what they're saying to each other.

"You know what your problem is? Randolph made you believe you control this whole situation, and you don't," a man who sounds older says.

"I control who comes in and out of this mansion. And you were uninvited." I inhale sharply. That's Jasper.

The other man laughs bitterly. "I'll own this place if you keep fucking around with me." He sounds like a wise guy.

I wait for Jasper to respond. Finally, he does, but his voice is so low that I can hardly make out what he's saying. I readjust my ear, hold my breath and really concentrate on their voices. That's when I hear Jasper say "journalist." Then he says my name.

"You don't think she knows who you are?" Jasper asks. "She sees you're a guest, and she'll start asking me questions."

"Why would she ask you questions?"

Jasper pauses and I take that brief moment to restore my breathing.

"Why is she here anyway?"asks the old man, who's obviously someone I might know.

"She's Bryn's friend."

"Get rid of her."

"As I said, Art, you don't control what goes on around here."

There's silence, the kind that signals a calm before the storm.

His name is Art?

"How's he doing anyway?" Art asks.

"Not well," Jasper replies. "He's on his last leg."

"Can I see him?"

"No." Jasper's tone is final. It's difficult to tell which man has the most power by the tone of their conversation.

"At some point, I'm going to have to know how he's progressing, you understand. And if he dies, I need to see the body."

Jasper's laugh has an edge. "You think I'm going to lie to you about my father dying?"

"Don't test me, kid. I'll destroy you. I'll start with that little sister of yours and I won't stop until every Blackstone is wiped off the face of this earth. You understand?"

I imagine Jasper standing tall, glaring at the man like an angry wolf. "Get the hell out of my house," Jasper finally growls.

"Your house?"

"Yes, my fucking house."

I wondered what happened. Did Jasper close the distance between him and Art? Is he towering over a more feeble specimen?

"I'll be in touch," Art says.

Art who?

If only I could get a look at Art. I hear a door open and close. That's my cue to get a move on. I don't want to be caught roaming these secret hallways. If Jasper finds me, he might expel me from the property. He wouldn't care that we're having great sex.

I barely reach the end of the corridor when I hear a door open. My heartbeats accelerate as I step into the first foyer I see, turn the knob on the door, which thankfully turns, and enter another tight, dark space.

There are voices, loud voices—I press my ear to the door, controlling my breathing. Footsteps, loud and deliberate, stomp down the hallway that I just abandoned. They stop right in front of the door I just walked through. *Oh no… please keep going Jasper, please.* Can he sense my presence?

Then I hear a loud bang and turn toward the noise. The sound comes from the room where voices commingle. Somehow, I feel Jasper has moved on. I tune out the heightened conversation on one side of me to listen for Jasper. Faintly, I can hear his footsteps. I sigh with relief. He's moving along.

"Stop you two," a woman screams. Then she lets out a loud wail.

I tense up, whipping my attention in their direction.

"What are you doing to yourself?" a man yells.

That's Asher.

"Leave us alone, Ash."

My eyes grow wide. *That's Spencer.*

My jaw drops as I gasp. It's all three of them together: Asher, Spencer, and could the woman be Gina?

There's banging. The woman cries, "Stop it."

It's Gina.

I hear more bumping and a series of thuds and bangs. Asher yells at Spencer, calling him selfish and sick. He says Spencer should get help and so should Gina.

Help for what?

"All right, it's time for you to cool off," Spencer says, sounding a lot more in control than Asher.

I pull the door open just a little and hold still when Gina and I connect gazes. She looks alarmed.

"Both of you leave, get out!" Gina exclaims.

Asher and Spencer continue to argue as their voices grow faint. Once I think they're gone, I open the door.

Gina's on the floor, looking like a broken doll. She's beyond shocked to see me as she continuously checks over her shoulder.

"What are you doing here?" she whispers.

Asher and Spencer haven't gone far. I'm too focused on Gina to make out exactly what they're saying. One side of her face is bruised. The right side of her top lip is swollen and bleeding.

What the hell…

I squat and take Gina by the arm. "Come with me."

At first, she looks conflicted, but as I pull her up,

she rises to her feet. We have to get out of this room and frankly out of this dark and dangerous house.

I have a one-track mind as we run, holding hands, down the hallway. She's able to keep up just fine, and the thought of that being odd for a woman who looks as if she's just been beaten badly passes through my mind, but still, all I can think about is escaping.

Sheer terror grips me as we race into Amelia's bedroom. The only thing on my mind is getting Gina far away from the house as fast as I can. My legs drive me past the two armchairs and to the door that leads to the visible hallway. I'm panting as I squeeze the knob, but something is wrong.

Gina is not following me. She's laughing and the sound makes me freeze. I whip myself around to see her slouched in an armchair, having a good old-fashioned belly laugh. I can hardly believe what I'm seeing, and that sentiment apparently shows on my face because she points at me as she continues cackling.

My mouth is stuck open, and all I can do is shake my head.

"Don't worry," Gina says. "I won't let them know you were there."

I jerk my head back. "What?"

"But I'm so impressed that you found your way to the rabbit hole."

"The rabbit hole?"

Only when she rises to her feet do I register that she's wearing racy lingerie which consists of a lacy black bralette and sheer panties.

"I told you that Spencer likes it rough. He likes it this rough because... Well, so do I. Asher's a boy, but Spencer's a man." Her eyes burn with lust and then anger. "And I don't want your pity, Reporter. Plus, I might look bad, but you should see the other guy."

"Because?" I say, my journalist's cap back on. At this point, I'm done playing nice with these people. I tried to feel for Gina, but she's just like the rest of them. She's a liar and she's hiding secrets, harmful secrets.

"Because?" she repeats.

"You said that Spencer likes it rough 'because'."

Gina shrugs indifferently.

I glare at her outfit again, realizing that it was Spencer who she was having an encounter with. I wonder if it was sexual. I wonder if he put his mouth on her.

"That bra..." I say.

She looks down at her tits. "What about it?"

"Did Spencer experience your tits?"

Her frown intensifies. "What do you mean by experience my tits?"

"Did he put his mouth on your tits while you were wearing that bra?"

The Night of the Christmas Party

HOLLY HENDERSON

I put the bra inside one of the plastic bags that I secured from the trashcan and then hide it with my shirt that contains Jasper's saliva. Now that those two items are safely tucked away, I take a moment to gather my bearings. All I need is Bryn's DNA and frankly I'm not sure she'll willingly let me have it.

And *Art?* Who is Art, and what's with the conversation he had with Jasper? The party will start soon so I enter the shower. The warm water soothes every inch of me as my brain struggles to figure out who this Art character is.

Art will more than likely be short for Arthur. I think of powerful men named Arthur who have

East Coast ties. A name and face come to mind and then I become paralyzed.

Of course it's him—Arthur Valentine, the multibillionaire political donor and a man who oozes slime. The connections begin to link in my head. Jasper is supposed to be running for President, although he never mentions it. And when I brought up the subject, the conversation was a dead end road. Did Jasper's father make a deal with Arthur Valentine? A deal that Jasper doesn't seem eager to satisfy.

I TAKE MY TIME GETTING READY FOR THE BIG EVENT. Bryn hadn't mentioned the Christmas party in her email. However, I did bring a few dresses just in case she wanted to join me for a night out on the town. I didn't know I would want to impress her eldest brother, though. Regardless, I think one of the dresses I brought will do.

I put on my black dress, which has a boat neck and three-quarter sleeves. I wish I were showing more skin but my dress fits snugly all the way down to the bend of my legs. I study myself in the standing mirror. My curves are on display. My hair is shiny and healthy. I look smart, elegant, and I think sexy too. Jasper will be pleased.

I put on my black patent leather Mary Jane heels, secure my matching cocktail purse where I put my wallet, cellphone, and a tube of red lipstick just in case I need to refresh, and walk out of the bedroom. I make my way to the party. Padding down the hallway, I feel so alone. I've felt alone in this part of the house ever since arriving. Now I know why. The others are hiding deep in the belly of the manor.

I follow the faint sound of instrumental holiday music until it starts to mingle with chatter. A smattering of women dressed in cocktail gowns and men in nice suits socialize in the hallways. Every single person I approach regards me with curiosity. Not just anyone receives an invitation to the annual Blackstone family holiday party. So I'm sure they are all wondering who I am and what sort of social capital I have to offer. I keep my head held high, though, fighting the urge to shrink and hide. I have no doubt that some might recognize me as the reporter who made a name out of taking down their powerful friends, the Howsleys.

I hope not.

That would be a disaster.

I increase my pace. The less time they have to figure out my identity, the less of a chance they will have to recognize me. Then, I enter a huge ballroom and I'm instantly taken aback by the number of guests. There have to be at least a few hundred. It's snowing and cold, but they still showed up.

Suddenly, I fold my arms over my chest, feeling like an ant under the heel of a shoe. But the decorations are supreme. I absorb all the columns, which are lit from within. The glow of light from each one creates a warm and festive ambiance. Chandeliers designed like round Christmas ornaments hang from the glass ceiling. Big open windows line the wall on one side of the ballroom, displaying a view of the sound, where lanterns float in the calm waters beyond the snow-covered lawn. A band plays the standards. People seem happy mingling. Conversation is spirited, bustling. It doesn't take long to notice a few high-profile politicos and billionaires in the room. None of them is Arthur Valentine.

I press my hand on my stomach when it growls. I'm hungry, but I also want to find Bryn and insist she level with me. My stomach continues to cramp from being starved. I catch sight of waiters in black-tie uniforms walking the floor, balancing trays of champagne and hors d'oeuvres with one hand. But the real score is behind the tables along the back wall, where real chefs cook up beautiful plates of food. I scope out a scallop dish and braised lamb chops for two. There are so many choices, and the way I feel right now, I want to try them all.

I'm making my way to the off-white bone china plates edged with gold when I see Jasper. He's standing in close proximity to a woman wearing a red dress. She has auburn hair and a beautiful figure. They seem quite cozy actually as his intense eyes settle on her face. He's looking at her as if she's the only person who matters to him and he's making sure he doesn't miss a word she speaks.

My heart takes a nosedive as I rip my gaze off of them and force myself to pretend as if they don't exist. He's such a liar, just like everybody else around here. I'm leaving tomorrow morning. *Fuck the Blackstones.*

"Do I know you?" A guy asks as he steps in front of me blocking my path.

It takes a moment to resolve some of my anger and disappointment so that I can bring his face more into focus. "I don't know. Do you know me?"

His giddy eyes lap my face. "I do know you,

Holly Henderson. But it seems you don't remember me. Take a guess."

I sigh impatiently. I don't want to guess. I want to eat. I want to clobber Jasper. I want to make a scene. However, I give it the old college try. The man is about my age. He's tall and nearly as handsome as Jasper with his tousled hair, sexy five o'clock shadow, and unserious but charismatic eyes.

"I know you as Bryn's college roommate," he says, graciously providing a hint.

I lean back to get a better look at him. She had so many guys coming in and out of her room, but there was only one I had shared a few conversations with.

My warms with recognition. "Dale Rumor?"

He opens his arms wide, ready to receive a hug. "Good guess."

"Oh my God," I say as we hug.

At least I now know who Bryn was screwing. His face beams with that sort of postsex glow. But why is she keeping him a secret? Instead of questioning him about his involvement with the current lady of the manor, I decide to play along.

"You look so Chris Hemsworth meets David Beckham," I say.

"Wow, that good, huh?" He laughs softly.

I chuckle. "That is a killer combination, isn't it?"

We share a laugh and then decide to get something to eat. As we walk, we talk about what he's up to these days. He says he's read both my books. *Odd... He doesn't seem like the type who indulges in unauthorized investigative biographies.*

After selecting our food, we find a cocktail table and sit. I try not to search for Jasper in the ballroom. But I am curious to know if he and the woman in the red dress decided to take their conversation to a cozier spot. Oh yes, he's a player. That's why he's so good at sex. I mean, he gave me an orgasm through my panties!

I focus intensely on Dale's face as he reveals that he clerked for an appellate court judge in Washington, DC, up until eight days ago. He recently decided that law wasn't for him. Instead, he's heading out to Los Angeles to start a career in television and film. Apparently, he's written a screenplay about a powerful family like the Blackstones. AEE, one of the most popular cable networks in the world, is interested in turning his story into a television series.

"You know, I can always use an advisor like you on my team. That book you wrote on the

Howsleys…" He pinches his thumb and forefinger together and shakes his hand. "That was an epic takedown."

I smile tightly. I'm so distracted. *Where is Jasper?*

"You don't agree with me?" he asks, perhaps reading my expression.

I sigh deeply, lassoing myself back to our conversation. "Sure." The takedown was definitely epic and well-deserved. The Howsleys were evil sons-of-guns. However, I don't want to talk about them. It's time to talk more about you, Dale. "So why are you here in Rhode Island? Did Bryn invite you?"

He abruptly leans across the table and now his face is closer. "If you don't mind my asking, how did your radar land on the Howsleys?"

I raise an eyebrow. He purposely ignored my question. Okay… I'll play along.

I smile wryly. "Interesting that you ask me that, counselor."

"Why is it interesting?"

"My sources are deep background. I'm pretty sure I mention that in the book. So you'll never get me to tell."

His lopsided smile is pretty attractive. "Very well."

I fold my arms tightly across my body and open my mouth to ask him yet again, what is the current nature of his association with Bryn.

"Dale," Jasper says as his hand comes crashing down hard on Dale's shoulder.

Dale twists his body to see the man standing behind him. He then hops off his stool to shake Jasper's hand. "Jasper, good to see you."

"You were invited, huh?" Jasper asks. His fake smile is scary enough to spook little children.

Dale does admit that he was invited by Bryn, who I spy walking into the ballroom. She's with a man who has dark hair and a killer smile. When I turn back to set my attention back to Dale, Jasper has shifted his position so I have to look around him to see the other man.

"Do you have a minute?" Jasper asks Dale with his back to me.

"Um…" Dale leans to the left to see me sitting behind Jasper.

"I want to talk to you about the Carmichael Trust case," Jasper says.

Dale smiles at me timidly. "Ah, yes, that. Well, you know I left Justice Nylander's stable."

Jasper's strong hand comes down on Dale's other shoulder. And now he has Dale in his grasp.

"That's okay. I'm sure you can still lend me some perspective."

"Sure. I could call you after the——"

"How about now?" Jasper says strongly.

Dale's eyes expand. "Now?"

"I won't be available after the holidays, so yes, now. I promise I won't take too much of your time."

Dale looks at me and raises a finger. "I'll be back. But just in case our paths don't cross later, which I'm going to make sure they do…" He takes his wallet out of his pocket and hands me his business card. "Let's grab drinks or dinner sometime. There's a lot I want to talk to you about."

Jasper removes his hands from Dale's shoulders as he twists around to glare at me. It's as if he's daring me to accept Dale's offer.

"Why not? Sure," I say with Dale's card pinched between my fingers. *This is for the woman in the red dress.*

Finally Jasper shifts to where he's not blocking my view of Dale. "We can talk in the cigar lounge."

Dale stretches his bottom lip squeamishly. "You mean *the* cigar lounge?"

Jasper glances at me uncomfortably. "Yes."

Dale studies Jasper with a narrowed eye as though he's assessing his intentions. Finally, Dale nods, and I watch the two of them walk off until they're swallowed up by crowds of people.

It's almost a relief that they're gone. I search the room for the woman in the red dress who Jasper was speaking to earlier. I can't seem to find her. Maybe she's waiting for him somewhere in this dastardly house. For a moment, I picture him doing to her what he did to me earlier today. I shake my head as I finish eating what's on my plate. I don't care who's looking either. I'm starving.

When I'm done eating, I stand and grab a glass of champagne off the tray of a passing waiter. It's time to find Bryn and make her answer some questions.

I take a few steps before out of nowhere William blocks my path.

"Excuse me, Miss Henderson, could you follow me, please?" he asks.

I frown at him. "Follow you where?"

"Mr. Blackstone asks that you meet him in a quieter setting."

I feel my grimace grow more intense. "Which Mr. Blackstone?"

"Mr. Jasper Blackstone," he says so low that I can barely hear him.

I sigh. I'm relieved he wants to be with me and not the woman in the red dress.

———————

A BLACK CAR WITH TINTED WINDOWS WAITS FOR ME at the back of the house. I can barely see it under the cover of night. William instructs me to walk down the steps and enter the back seat. After I do what I'm told. I wonder where I'm being taken. I know wherever I end up, Jasper will be waiting.

The distance is short because I've been driven as far as the guest cottage. The driver hurries out of the front seat to open my door. And now, like a moth stung by the flame, my body burns with need.

The front door is cracked and I open it. The fireplace crackles, and it's cozy inside. Suddenly, two arms wrap me up from behind and hard body parts press against me. His hypnotic scent overtakes me.

"Jasper?" I sigh.

His minty breath warms my ear. "Don't ever do that again." He spins me around and now I'm gazing hazily at his beautiful face.

"Do what?" I whisper, my throat weighted down by desire.

"What you were doing with Dale."

"Talking to him," I say as if that was obvious.

"You took his business card. Do you still have it?"

I looked down at my cocktail purse. Then I close my eyes and sigh gravely. "Damn it. I left it on the…" But then I remember that I had absent-mindedly stuffed it in my bosom. I reach in and pull it out. "No, it's here."

Eyes narrowed to slits, Jasper takes the card from me and with his elegant gait, strolls over and pitches the card into the fireplace.

"Are you serious?" I ask as he heads back toward me.

"I'm serious."

I'm in his arms. I feel as light as a feather fluttering to the earth as our mouths meld. Then I'm off my feet and we're still kissing as Jasper carries me to his bed.

WE ROLL ALL OVER HIS BED. SLOWLY BUT SURELY our clothes come off. The act of kissing, petting, squeezing, sucking, and biting makes us glisten with sweat. And now, we can't hold off any longer. Jasper is on top of me, his hips between my thighs and my legs around him, my ankles crossed, locking him against me. We are playing with fire.

"When was the last time you slept with a prostitute?" I ask, figuring it's time to have the conversation before I let him inside me without protection.

His hands sinking into the mattress, he holds himself up. "A what?"

Goodness, Jasper Blackstone has the most intimidating frown. But I'm not backing down.

"Prostitute," I say more clearly.

"Why are you asking me if I have sex with prostitutes?"

It's time to give a little away, to bait my hook and see how much he bites. "I spent yesterday afternoon with Gina at the swimming pool, and she said that she was a prostitute and the two of you had an encounter."

He blinks at me without any sort of discernible expression. "Babe, I haven't had sex with a woman in a long time," he says in a tone that's almost a whisper. Then he smirks. "Not before you arrived at least. And I certainly have never fucked Gina."

My heart feels drenched by his sincerity. "I hadn't done it in a long time either," I admit. "I mean, it's been over a year."

"I've been tested for every disease in the book," he says. "What about you?"

"Same," I say breathlessly.

He grins naughtily. "Then let's do it raw."

Damn, that sounds sexy. It sounds hot. Explicit. How can I say no? And then I gasp as his thick erection breaks through me.

HOURS LATER

Our skin is wet and so are the sheets. However, it suddenly occurs to me that Jasper Blackstone and I are spooning. Of course he's the big spoon, a man like him wouldn't have it any other way. Our closeness doesn't feel weird either. On the contrary, it's as if being this close to him is where I belong.

"So how did this happen?" I ask.

"What do you mean?"

"You left the ballroom with Dale to have a cigar and a talk, but you got here before I did. I figured a conversation about the Carmichael Trust would last longer than that."

He chuckles against me, and I love feeling his

whole body shake with laughter. "You're always fishing, aren't you?"

I *am* fishing. "I'm not fishing."

"Yes, you are. But it's fine. I like that about you. I knew he worked on the case against the Carmichael Trust, but I had no questions. I wanted to get him away from you."

I laugh as I nestle myself deeper against his body. I don't know, for some reason, and maybe it's because all of the sex we've been having in the past three days, but I feel as if I belong to him. "So Dale and Bryn are still friends?" I'm fishing again.

"They've never been friends." He answered that without measuring his response. Also, I'm pretty certain he has no love for Dale, none whatsoever.

"But he used to always come to our dorm to see her. They would spend the night together too."

Jasper's body tenses up against me. After a few beats, he says, "Dale is Asher's friend."

I frown confused. "No. He used to come to our dorm room at least twice a week to see Bryn. They'd go to her bedroom and lock themselves up for hours."

He grunts thoughtfully. "Is that so?" I find his response pretty lacking. Especially since he just learned that a man he obviously doesn't like had indeed been involved with his sister during college.

"You didn't know?" I ask.

He pauses. "No, I didn't."

How could he not know? Jasper is the master of all their universes. Surely he knows about Bryn and Dale. *He's lying. Why?*

"I find that hard to believe," I finally say.

"Believe it." Then in a brand new tone he says, "Listen, I don't want you talking to that guy."

"Dale?" I ask my voice ringing with surprise.

"Yes."

"Why not?"

"He likes you."

A laugh that connotes how ridiculous that sounds escapes me. But Jasper does not laugh.

"What about the woman in the red dress?" I ask. "You looked pretty into her?"

He stiffens as if he just jerked his head in surprise. "Are you talking about Susan?" I don't know if he sounds shocked or offended.

"Is that her name?"

"Yes. And she's my employee. We were discussing business. And just so you know, she's married with three kids, and her husband is also at the party."

I feel like shrinking from embarrassment. "Oh," I barely say.

Then, something inside me wants to test our potential for a relationship that goes beyond my stay at the Blackstone mansion. "Well, I won't be single for all my life. And Dale's cute and kind of successful too," I say, even though I suspect Dale is the one who had been banging Bryn before the party.

"Are you fucking kidding me?" he hisses.

I shake my head against the pillow. "What do you want from me, Jasper? You're the one who snuck into my room and then you screwed me in this bed yesterday morning. Then there was last night. Oh, not to mention your office. While I'm here, you've been running our show, Jasper. But when I'm gone, you don't have a say."

He's very quiet and very still. I wait with bated breath for him to say something. I half expect Jasper to release me and make an excuse to send me away. Instead, he plants a tender kiss on my shoulder. "I didn't expect this to happen between us," he whispers. "I don't…"

I wait for him to finish whatever he's going to say. It soon becomes apparent he's not going to finish.

"You don't what?" I ask in an eager voice.

"I have a lot of obligations, Holly."

I recall his conversation with Arthur Valentine. "What sort of obligations?"

Even though he has nothing to say, the tension in his body speaks loudly. I wonder if I should mention Arthur Valentine. There's no way to do it without admitting that I've been sneaking around the secret hallways. However, this is the first time since we began our hot and heavy rendezvousing that Jasper has been this open with me. Now is the time to keep it going.

"Are you still thinking about running for president in the next election? I mean, first you have to get past the primaries, but I'm sure you have people who can help you with that?"

He's on the move.

I'm on my back.

He's between my knees.

My thighs.

"Not if I can help it," he whispers lustfully.

I press my head back against the pillow when his warm and soft mouth makes contact with my sweet clam.

The Truth But Not The Whole Truth

HOLLY HENDERSON

DECEMBER 24TH

I slowly open my eyes. The room is filled with bright light from the glare of the snow shining in through the window. The night of sex, no, making love, comes rushing back to me like the winds of a storm. I sit up. I'm alone in bed, but I fell asleep in Jasper's embrace.

"Jasper?" I call.

There's no answer.

I call again, louder and wait. Still, only silence brews in the air. If he hadn't held me, kissed my shoulder, and refused to let go of me, then I would feel cheap. But I don't feel cheap. Jasper Blackstone is a busy man and I'm a busy woman.

I have plans for today. It's Christmas Eve, so I have to get to the UPS Store early. Without further delay, I put on my clothes and rush out of the guesthouse.

It snowed more last night and the chill in the air strangles my lungs. I wonder why Jasper didn't say goodbye before he left. But then I see the answer as I trudge up the snow cleared path. Parked in front of the house is an ambulance casting its lights against the grim day. I'm certain the ambulance and Jasper's early rising has something to do with his father's failing health.

JUST LIKE THE PREVIOUS MORNINGS, I RETURN TO my bedroom without being noticed. I quickly take off my party dress and put on long spandex workout pants, a T-shirt, a zip-up hoodie, and running shoes. I hurry to the bathroom to wash the remains of last night's makeup off my face and then tie my hair into a ponytail.

"There," I say, studying my reflection in the mirror. Appearing as if I'm going out for a run is the perfect cover.

"Where were you last night?"

I jump and see Bryn's reflection standing in the doorway. I quickly turn to face her.

"There you are." I'm actually surprised to see her. From day one, I thought I'd be seeing a lot more of her. But that has not been the case.

Her face is blotchy, and the skin beneath her eyes are puffy. "Where have you been?"

"Here!" I answer a little too excitedly. "I went to the party last night. It was lovely." I'm trying to throw her off my trail.

She continues to stare at me intensely, coldly. "I know. I saw you, but then you were gone."

I cross then uncross my arms. Why am I so nervous? "Yeah, well... I'm working for you. Remember?"

She snorts bitterly. "You weren't in your room last night, Holls."

I shake my head softly. There's no use denying it.

"You're not screwing Jasper, are you?"

My mouth is caught open. One word comes to my head for some reason. "No," I say even though I don't want to lie.

Her smile is bitter. "You're lying. Were you with him last night?"

I curl my top lip. "I guess I'm joining the club. Everybody lies around here. Even the butler."

She takes brisk steps to stand next to me. "I told you to stay away from him." She's whispering again.

"I know," I whisper. "But I can't stay away from him. I like him. I'm attracted to him. We have chemistry."

Bryn's eyes scour my face. Her expression is a mixture of empathy and real concern.

"What?" I blurt.

"I knew he was attracted to you." She sighs softly, shaking her head. "Come. Let's sit."

I feel as if I'm walking in an alternate universe as I follow Bryn to the high-backed chairs. I have no doubt that what she's going to say to me will not feel good.

"The only thing Jasper can do for you is hurt you, Holls," she says.

I frown, recalling last night and what he said about continuing to date me, to see where these feelings we have for each other take us.

"Listen," she says before I can come up with a response. "I'm supposed to marry someone."

I pause my thoughts to examine her. "Dale Rumor?"

"No," she says quietly. "It's someone else."

"Who is it?"

"But Dale and I are seeing each other," she says.

I know she heard my question but she has a way, like Jasper, of picking and choosing what she'll respond to. I've already sussed out that I might never get the name of the man she's being forced to marry—not if I don't play my cards right.

I clear my throat and readjust in my seat. "And Jasper doesn't know about you and Dale, does he?"

"No… Maybe…" She flings her hand. "I don't care."

A direct answer to a direct question—perfect.

I narrow an eye curiously. "And I suspect Dale is the one who told you there's something going on between Jasper and me?"

"Yes, he did. And Dale also said that Jasper was infuriated to see the two of you talking."

I roll my eyes. "Yeah, well, I don't understand why you would keep the fact that you're in a relationship with Dale from your brother."

"I told you why."

I lean forward. "Because he doesn't like Dale?"

Her shoulders fall limp at the bottom of her sigh. "It's more than that. It's…"

I wait for her to finish, but I can feel the angst

emanating from her. "You can tell me, Bryn. Come on. I'm on your side, here."

"Are you?" she snaps. "Because you're screwing the one person who—"

I scoot to the edge of my seat. "The one person who?" I ask leadingly.

She runs her fingers through her hair then falls back in her seat. "Jasper. He's spoken for, Holls."

I stare at her but she's fallen out of focus. "He's spoken for?" I'm barely able to ask.

"Our family has debts."

Debts, spoken for—it's too much to consume at once. "Debts?"

"That's why you're here. I know you will give up on this if Jasper breaks your heart. And he will, Holls. He will."

I'm lost for words. My insides feel as if they've morphed into a substance more solid than steel, and that instant feeling of being unbreakable allows me to find my voice.

"He won't hurt me," I claim, jaw set. "He can't because I won't let it happen." I mean what I say. I know how to be tough. You don't have a childhood like I had and then wither from something as mediocre as heartbreak. So I sit tall in my chair, refocus on what's important, and look Bryn directly in the eyes and ask, "Listen, do you know Arthur Valentine?"

She stiffens as if that name just slapped her in the face. "Yes."

"He's a bad guy."

"I know." This time it sounds like she's whispering because her throat is tight.

"Why would he be in your house?"

Bryn closes her eyes which twitch as they try to hold back the tears that have started sliding down her cheeks.

"Carter Valentine… I'm supposed to marry him." She swallows. "But I can't."

I stifle a sigh of relief. Good… I got her to tell me what I've been fishing for.

"Arthur Valentine's son?" I ask.

She nods stiffly.

I've heard of him. I've also heard that Carter is nothing like his father which is something Arthur's not happy about.

I grunt thoughtfully. "Doesn't Arthur have a daughter?"

"Victoria."

Then it hits me, the fist of illumination. The way Bryn stares into my eyes as if she's confirming my guess. But I can't ask her to just say it. I don't want to hear it.

I sigh and purse my lips, feeling the impact of being in this house for the past four days. "There are dark hallways in this mansion. Your brothers are sharing one woman, and one of them hits her, and I think she hits him too. You're supposed to marry a Valentine and so is Jasper who's supposedly running for president one day. And your mother…"

Not until I mentioned Amelia does Bryn seem interested in what I'm saying which makes me suspect that her mother is indeed the main reason why I was invited to the Blackstone mansion in the first place.

Bryn scoots to the edge of her seat and then leans toward me. "What about Amelia?"

"Well, one of my sources revealed your mother's real age."

Bryn's eyebrows shoot up. "Which source?"

I shake my head. "I always protect my sources. You know that. However, I'll provide you concrete evidence if you're still interested."

"I'm interested."

"Your mother was forty-two when she died."

Bryn's eyes grow wide with surprise.

"How old did you think she was?"

She can't stop shaking her head. "Older than forty-two."

"You never knew your mother's age?"

"No."

And now it's time to ask for what I need from her. "Bryn, can you provide me with a sample of your DNA?"

Her eyes widen as if she's afraid of what I'm asking her to do.

Then we're both jolted as there's a knock on the doorjamb. We turn to see Jasper filling the frame.

Bryn and I both receive his careful attention. He knows he's walked in on a moment between us, perhaps something he would not approve of.

"Bryn, we need you downstairs," he says, eyebrows pinched.

"For what?" She sounds annoyed.

"Our father just died. And we're paying our respects together."

She rolls her eyes and after a weary sigh, rises to her feet. Without another word she pads out of the room, leaving me hanging. I need her DNA. I don't think she wants to give it to me.

Now that she's gone it's just Jasper and me. I have so much to say to him, so many accusations to hurl at him. But then he smiles, a real happy to be alone with me smile, and that catches me off guard.

My pulse races as I gape at him. "He's dead? Your father?"

"Yes," Jasper says and closes the door behind him. Then he's standing in front of me, beckoning me to rise to my feet. I stand and then our lips connect, and his needy tongue indulges in mine. Holding me close and moaning into my mouth, Jasper kisses me as if his life depends on it.

"How about we get the hell out of here tonight?" he asks between kisses.

My eyes expand in disbelief as our tongues and lips continue their deep exploration of each other. After what I've learned about him, how could he ask me that? Finally, our mouths take a break.

"Get out of here tonight?" I whisper out of breath. "And go where?"

His eyes gleam with something I've never seen from him before and then he closes them to dream. "Anywhere in the world. You name it."

His lips chase mine as I lean back.

"Jasper, open your eyes." My brisk tone is designed to bring him back to the moment.

It seems like an arduous task for him to raise his eyelids, but he does it.

"I'm sorry to hear about your father," I say, remaining levelheaded.

After a few beats, he stands up straight and clears his throat. "I'm sorry." His frown crushes my heart but at least he sounds more like himself.

I frown too, but in concern more than anger. "It's okay."

"Will you please have breakfast in your room this morning? We have family affairs to discuss downstairs."

I nod softly. "Of course." I wouldn't dare intrude.

Jasper bows his head and calmly walks to the door and opens it. Then he turns back, and his penetrating gaze takes me in. My heart skips a beat. "I'll see you later, Holly. We have to talk."

I resist the urge to bring up Julia Valentine and nod.

———

Now that I'm alone, I rush to the closet, and open my suitcase. It's empty. Gina's bra is gone and... What the hell. My panties have been washed and folded. I look up at my clothes hanging on the bar. The shirt that had Jasper's saliva on it has been laundered.

I want to scream. But instead I press my balled fists against my temples and squeeze my eyes shut tightly.

I'm thinking fast.

All the Blackstones are downstairs, discussing their father's death. They're eating breakfast.

"They're eating breakfast?" I stand out of my squat.

It's time for Plan C.

The Final Collection

HOLLY HENDERSON

I roam down hallways, avoiding William and Nigel, the butlers, but looking for any other house staff. I encounter two people in the ballroom, cleaning up from last night's party. They tell me where I can find Crystal Preacher. She's in the laundry room with two other maids. They are all engaged in a spirited conversation about the guests who attended last night's party. Once they catch sight of me, they all stand at attention, and Crystal asks if there's something she can assist me with.

"Actually, yes." I ask for a moment alone with her.

The look on her face shows that she's slightly ambivalent and a little intrigued. However, she agrees to step into the hallway with me. Once I'm sure no one can hear us, I ask if she could do me a big favor.

---

45 MINUTES LATER

I turn to glance into the back seat of my car. Four porcelain coffee cups sit on the seat staring back at me. Crystal had gone into the kitchen and collected the cups from Jasper, Bryn, Asher, and Spencer's morning coffee. She even packaged each in their own Ziploc bag and wrote the name of each sibling on the plastic with a permanent marker. She had been quite thorough, and I thanked her for it.

Now I'm driving back to Providence. Sure, there are stores in Newport, but the farther away I am from the Blackstones' reach, the safer I feel about my delivery actually making it to the lab in California. One of them got rid of the samples I had already collected. I know this because Gina's bra was missing. Who was it? Bryn? Jasper? Spencer? Asher? All of them? I can't pinpoint a culprit, not yet at least.

I want to make sure no one is following me.

Every now and then, I'll check my rearview mirror. Today's unfortunate development makes now the optimal time to run my errand. Randolph Blackstone has died. *Gosh, he's dead.* Neither Jasper nor Bryn seem sad about it.

I think about the death of my own mother. I'd never broke down and cried about her passing. Perhaps deep beneath the surface, like Bryn, I had a lot of anger toward my mother, Gayle Henderson. She allowed my father to drag us from one state to another and from one bad situation to a worse one. It has taken me years to forgive her and my dad for just being two fallible human beings who should've never had a kid together.

I catch a quarter-view glimpse of my face in the rearview mirror as I drive into the crowded parking lot of the UPS store. I resemble my mother. We have the same eyes, thick and long dark-brown hair, and a heart-shaped face. I run my hand gently cross my cheek. For the first time ever, I love seeing my mom's face reflecting back at me through a mirror. I don't know why, but I do.

I find a parking spot, turn off my engine, and take my samples inside to be safely mailed and on their way to California.

NEARLY AN HOUR AND A HALF LATER, I'M RELIEVED to be out of the UPS Store and on my way back to the mansion. Goodness, the UPS Store had been a circus. People were shipping last-minute gifts which reminded me that I hadn't bought anything for the Blackstones. Yes, they are wealthy and probably have everything already, but I have come to know their little quirks. Maybe I can offer them a little cheer since their father died.

I search for the nearest shopping mall and drive to the department store. All men love a good tie, after rummaging through the many colors and patterns, I finally select one for Asher and one for Spencer. A pair of cuff links catch my attention. They have an onyx stone surrounded by encrusted diamonds and gold. The cuff links remind me of all the unique facets of Jasper—his intensity, elegance, darkness, and undeniable sex appeal. They're expensive, but I splurge and buy them for him anyway.

Bryn is the hardest to shop for. She's so secretive and I can't fathom why. I have to admit that I hardly know her at all. She's still so much like that young girl who walked into the auditorium on the first day we met and chose me because I didn't know her family. I've been at her house for four days and we haven't done something together once. Real friends shop together, sightsee together, enjoy a walk together, and more. I ponder what I would want a friend like Bryn to give me for Christmas. Then it comes to mind, and I buy that gift. I wonder how Bryn will receive it.

It's late afternoon when I make it back to the Blackstone manor. The ambulance is long gone, but the estate has a different vibe. The air feels lighter. The lights in the trees twinkle brighter. The place carries an aura that makes me feel as though I'm coming home.

I clench the steering wheel and remind myself the brightness and the holiday ambiance are a disguise. All of them keep rooms that are part of the dark hallways, all except Jasper. He stays in the guest cottage. I don't think Jasper loves being inside the manor. That's why he suggested that we run away together. *Run away from what?*

I open the garage door and pull into the stall. After turning the engine off, I sit with my eyes closed for a moment. I have to put everything I've discovered while being here into perspective. On day one, Bryn had mentioned that her mother would not apologize for being a horrible parent. *Hell, join the club.* However, today I learned that Bryn is supposed to marry a man she doesn't love. Jasper is promised to a woman he doesn't love either. I hope he doesn't love her. Maybe he's with me, sowing his wild oats.

No...

He's not the type.

But he was in Amelia's room when I arrived. That was odd. He was just sitting there alone, staring out the window. I felt the melancholy he left behind. *What was that about?*

I rub my temples to alleviate the tightness in my head. My instincts, reason, and emotions are at war with each other. Then there's the brush Sally gave me. She knows something, but she won't say. *Why not?*

Knock, knock, knock.

I jump because I recognize the cadence of the sound. *Gosh... I know his knock?* I look out the driver's side window, and Jasper takes a step back. He doesn't look happy to see me. I sigh wearily and get out of the car. It's so cold.

"Where were you?" he asks.

"Running some errands," I snap as I use the

remote mechanism on my keychain to open the trunk.

"What sort of errands?"

"Follow me," I say as I walk to the back of my car.

I lift the lid of my trunk and open my shopping bag. "Tomorrow's Christmas, and I hadn't bought anything for your family. I thought—"

"Damn it. I'm an asshole," he says. "I'm sorry for confronting you this way. I thought…"

I gaze at his handsome face with unyielding focus. "You thought what?"

He takes a deep breath as if savoring the scent that's emanating from me. "You being gone had something to do with Dale Rumor."

A bewildered laugh escapes me. "You really don't know, do you?"

He grimaces. "What don't I know?"

"Bryn and Dale are involved, Jasper. They're in love."

Jasper's expression moves from surprise to anger.

I figure there's no time like the present to mention his obligation to another woman. "And you're supposed to marry Julia Valentine."

He blinks rapidly and then gapes at me with a

pained and watery-eyed gaze. It's odd, I've never seen Jasper like this before. It's as if he has nothing to say about it.

We stand in silence for few beats which feel like they linger for far too long. It's as if I can discern that it just turned darker than it was a second ago.

"I'm not marrying her," he says tightly.

"But aren't you..."

"No," he blurts, cutting me off.

"You don't have to worry about Julia. I'm not marrying her and Bryn's not marrying Carter."

I wait for him to say more but he sets his jaw as if he's spoken. But I can see the strain in his eyes and on his face. He's made the claim but he's aware of how arduous it's going to be to bring it to pass. *Arthur Valentine.* I've had a run-in with him before, and I don't want to ever run into him again.

I shake my head and then dig his gift out of the bag. "This is for you. I'm going to bed. Don't come in my room tonight." I grab my purse and slam my trunk closed.

Before I can walk away from him, Jasper seizes me from behind and draws me against his solid physique. I close my eyes as I feel the electricity his nearness sets off inside me race through me.

"Please don't ban me from your room. I need you, Holly."

I can feel through his pants how much he needs me. My heart throbs like his manhood. It's too late to resist Jasper Blackstone. I won't even try. I'll be gone soon anyway.

"Okay," I barely say.

His chest rises and lowers as he sighs.

Mouth next to my ear, he says, "Join us for Christmas Eve dinner. I want to see your pretty face at the table."

Practicing no restraint whatsoever, I quickly spin on my heels. My lips are against his. My tongue is in his mouth and then his is in mine. I drop my bag and now we're making out feverishly, not caring who sees us.

The Freed Blackstones

HOLLY HENDERSON

J asper and I enter the house. We constantly glance at each other with flirtatious smiles and come hither eyes as we walk through the hallways. Then we enter a living room area which is near the ballroom where last night's party had been held. The space is large and designed to look like a modern living room spread in *Town & Country Magazine*. Strings of gold lights are draped around a large Christmas tree, which is minimally but tastefully decorated with blue, gold, and white satin bulbs. Presents all wrapped in the same gold paper lie at the foot of the tree. I'm surprised there are so many.

"Holly bought gifts," Jasper says, holding up my shopping bag.

All of his siblings regard us with weary expressions. Asher sits on one side of the sofa and Bryn on the other. She's sipping a glass of wine while bad posture has her positioned at the edge of the cushion. Asher has his thumbs pressed against his temples as if he's nursing a migraine. Spencer downs a glass of what looks like strong liquor and then slams his glass on the bar top.

I do a double take of him. Beneath his right eye is faint purpling. He's covered bruising. *Holy shit!*

"Put them under the tree," Bryn says in a dull voice.

"She'll give them to you now. And you'll open them and be thankful," Jasper says brusquely.

I don't think he's reading the room very well. Or, he's such a control freak that he doesn't care to read the room.

"I'm leaving," Asher announces. He's on his feet and sweeps past his eldest brother so fast that Jasper is lost for words to stop him.

I have a feeling that they were all engaged in a heavy conversation before Jasper and I showed up.

"We have to discuss our next steps. But after dinner," Jasper says and then walks over to put my presents under the tree. The festive wrapping that I paid for looks foreign against the other golden wrapped presents.

"Do what you want," Bryn says as she bounds to her feet. "And I'm not hungry." She looks at Jasper forlornly. "He's dead, Ace. This is over. We're free."

Jasper seems to be stuck in place as he watches Bryn sashay out of the room. There's something about her energy that makes me want to go after her. But I stay put for now.

Finally, Spencer walks over to the tree, bends down next to Jasper's long legs and finds the gift I bought him. He opens the box, takes out the tie and holds it in front of his face to inspect it.

My stomach is queasy and chest tight. I feel so humiliated until he pulls the corners of his mouth downward to nod and say, "Good taste, Journalist." He drapes the tie over his broad shoulder and then stares daggers at me. "By the way, you should stay out of the tunnels. You never know what might happen to you in there."

"Enough," Jasper barks.

Spencer's smirk is more of a snarl as he saunters out of the grand space with the tie that I bought him still draped over his shoulder. He's just left Jasper and me alone.

The tension in the air is still thick as Jasper looks at me with something inscrutable in his eyes. It certainly isn't lust, and it surely isn't love.

"You were in the tunnels?" he asks in a low, growling voice.

I swallow hard. There's no need to lie. "Yes, I was."

"What were you doing in the tunnels?"

I stand a bit taller. "Searching."

His kissable lips are so tight that they've thinned out. "Searching for what?"

I'm staring into his eyes, seeking warmth. I think I see it hiding behind disappointment, weariness and yes, sadness.

"Whatever I could find," I reply.

Jasper's hard expression doesn't waver. "Go upstairs, please. I'll have dinner brought to your room. I'll send the servers up."

"Are you banishing me to my room?" I ask feeling defensive.

"No," he says with a tender voice.

I gape at him. I want to ask if I'll see him later or confirm that we're finally done pretending that we can take whatever this is between us beyond my stay at the manor. But instead, I nod and walk away from him with tears burning the backs of my eyes.

But I walk through Amelia's bedroom, and then through the cabinet, into the tunnels and straight to the room where I heard Bryn and Dale getting it on. She and I—we have a lot to talk about.

———

I KNOCK.

"It's me, Holly, open up." I incline my ear toward the door. I can't hear a thing. Maybe she's escaped deeper into the dark tunnels. I decide to count to ten before entering without being invited in. I arrive at three when the door opens.

Only Bryn's face is visible. She's hiding the rest of her behind the door.

"Are you naked?" I ask.

She pulls the door back wider, giving me space to pass. I enter and look her up and down. She's all legs and a long slender body while wearing only panties and a bra. But then I look around. Her room is a mess. Clothes are strewn everywhere. Makeup and perfume are messy on top of a large dresser. Her bed is unmade. It's as though the maids have never come in to clean. Maybe they don't know about this part of the manor. Maybe they're not allowed in the tunnels.

"Well, listen, I've decided to stay out of your family affairs," I say.

She laughs bitterly as she races into her walk-in closet. "Whatever, Holly." Bryn comes back with a suitcase and tosses it on top of her bed.

I'm flabbergasted. "Going somewhere?"

"It's too late," she says hopping into a pair of jeans and then roughly putting on a thick sweater.

I frown. "What do you mean?"

"You know too much about us. Jasper feels he has to manage you now." She walks over to a drawer and pulls it out. "That's what having sex with you was all about, Holls. He's a control freak. But not anymore. Randolph is dead. We'll be running our own lives from this point onward."

At least now I know what the siblings were talking about before Jasper and I showed up.

Bryn gathers a handful of panties and bras. I don't think she's in complete control of her emotions. Her anxiety is so strong that it's poking me in the eyes.

"Bryn." I walk over and put a hand on her shoulder. "Calm down."

She shakes her head erratically. "You don't know what's about to happen. Randolph is dead. I'm not marrying Carter."

"Okay, but let's take a breather and discuss this first. You know I'm good at that, strategic thinking."

Bryn sighs then looks me deeply in the eyes. "Oh, Holls…" She gently rubs the side of my face. "The men in my family are damaged. Go home. Go home tonight and forget my brother ever existed. I'll be in touch." She slips into tall fashionable boots.

Her words hit me so hard that I jerk back. "What do you mean by damaged?"

"They don't know how to love because nobody ever loved them. And I'm nothing but an asset to them. I'm getting as far away from this house as I possibly can." She rushes back over to the dresser, picks up her phone, and makes a call.

I have no idea how to talk her off this ledge.

Apparently, whoever she's calling doesn't pick up, so she calls again and again. Finally, she whips her face around and scalds me with her glare. "Did you tell Jasper about Dale and me?"

"No." The look in her eyes made me lie.

"You better not have." She put the phone on speaker then takes another load of clothes and drops it into the suitcase. The operator's voice says the phone is no longer in service.

"Are you trying to call Dale?" I ask.

"I don't know what happened to his number. When I get to the airport, I'll check email on my laptop. I have to go." She shoots past me again.

I shake my head in shock. "Airport? Where are you going?"

This moment is way too surreal.

"I'm not telling you. You're sleeping with the enemy."

"Your brother is not your enemy Bryn. He said…" I stop myself from telling her that Jasper said Bryn will never marry Carter. She's not in the right mindset to hear it. "Do you want me to drive you to the airport?"

Her laugh is hard, brittle. "No way. You stay here and keep Jasper off my ass."

I sit on the foot of her messy bed as she keeps racing around the room throwing items into her disheveled suitcase.

"Bryn, do you think Dale is avoiding your call? Because if so—"

"No," she snaps. "We have a plan." She closes her suitcase.

"What sort of plan?"

She snatches her luggage by the handle. "I have to go. By the way, what did you get me?"

I'm confused. "Get you?"

"The Christmas gift."

"Oh." I'm relieved she asked. "Chocolates by Dauphine Chocolatier."

Bryn smiles slightly. "Thank you. I don't eat chocolate, but if things hadn't gone this way, I would've ordered up a couple of bottles of wine and let you eat them while I drank."

I'm still absorbing what else she's saying when she rushes into the bathroom. I think it was goodbye and that she'll get in touch with me when it's safe.

"Safe?" I call after her.

I hear what sounds like a door swing open and then close. Suddenly, I have that familiar feeling of being alone in this house. She's gone.

Our Night

HOLLY HENDERSON

I'm back in Amelia's bedroom, standing at the window, looking out over the darkened grounds. I wonder if I should wait until morning to get the hell out of Dodge or go now. I'm fine with leaving Jasper, sort of. I'll miss him. I'll miss him a lot.

"You're still here?" Jasper says, his voice tempered with relief and something else.

I sigh, composing myself and then turn around to see him. Why does it feel as if I've been gazing into his eyes this way since the beginning of time? What a handsome man he is. They say he's dangerous, and I can see the danger in him. But I can also see that he's capable of love—deep, unceasing, unconditional love.

"Hi," barely ekes out of my mouth.

Jasper and I continue to stare silently into each other's eyes. I wonder if he's having the same reaction to me that I'm having to him.

I point my hand at the chairs. "Can we sit and talk?"

He hesitates, then we both take a seat at the same time. Our knees and legs touch, though. He feels warm, alive. However, for the first time ever, I notice every single line of stress he wears on his face. Even though he's a youthful-looking man, the threat of appearing aged before his time nips at his heels. I want to touch his skin, kiss his cheek, and whisper, "I'll help you," in his ear. I'll help him be happy. I'll help him stay calm, feel safe. I'll be the one person who will never abandon him, leave him alone to pick up the pieces after the walls come tumbling down. But it's time to come clean with Jasper—completely clean.

I take a steadying sigh and smile slightly, hoping my expression would affect him. It doesn't.

"As you know, I've been doing some investigating while here. However, I ended up with more questions than answers, like the mystery surrounding your mother's age. I learned she was forty-two when she passed, which would've only made her fourteen, going on fifteen years old when she gave birth to you."

I pause, waiting for him to say something. Instead, he purses his lips as though he's waiting to find out how much more I know.

I clear my throat and push down the feeling of wanting to run as far away from Jasper as possible. He can be quite intimidating. "My source provided me with your mother's DNA. I'll be able to match the results with other samples I sent to the lab— samples of your DNA and your siblings."

My chest is tight as I wait for him to say something or for his expression to stop being so damn unreadable. But he changes nothing.

"How do you feel about that?" I ask to get him talking.

"I feel as though I let you into my house, knowing that you are a top investigative journalist. Therefore, I'm not shocked by what you're saying to me." His voice has an edge to it.

"Okay," I say, unsure if he's complimenting me or condemning me. I readjust in my chair. "Did you ever know your mother's actual age?"

"According to you, I didn't."

Okay… "Well, how old did you think she was?" I shoot back quickly, giving him no time to consider whether or not he should answer my question.

Jasper crosses and uncrosses his legs and then strokes his chin thoughtfully. "Not as young as you say she was. I don't know. I never thought about my mother's age. She never celebrated birthdays. The thought of getting older frightened the hell out of Amelia, actually."

"And what about Arthur Valentine?" I ask.

He sits up straight. "What about him?"

"You already know I was roaming through the tunnels. I overheard you having a conversation with Arthur Valentine. First of all, was it *the* Arthur Valentine?" I already know it was, but it would be nice for Jasper to confirm it.

He nods sharply. "If you're referring to Arthur Bradley Valentine, then yes."

I frown. "What sort of debt do you owe him?"

Jasper's jaw flexes as he looks off. Gosh, what a killer profile he has. "I can't say."

I haven't become such a good journalist by backing down, and I'm not going to start now. "Okay, then *why* do you owe him a debt?"

Jasper snorts a bitter laugh. "Same question, Miss Henderson."

My eyes grow wide. "Miss Henderson?" I sound and feel so disappointed.

He winks at me. "For now."

I laugh softly as I smile a little. I sit up straight and resume my interrogation of the one and only Jasper Blackstone. I'm probably the only person in the world who's ever gotten to do this, and boy, is it turning me on.

"But would you believe me if I told you I don't know what that debt is my father owes Valentine?"

I rub my face where my skin feels flushed. "I don't know," I say breathily. I'm breaking composure. I have to get a grip.

His eyes narrow. However, they've turned glossier, making it easier to see the emotion behind them. "As kids, we were taught a lot of things. We were never supposed to question the logic behind the lessons. They were just what they were. My father owed a debt to Arthur, a debt I'm still supposed to make good on."

"And you never asked what that debt was?"

"As I said, you don't question Randolph Blackstone."

I've come across plenty of rich, powerful, and narcissistic men like Jasper's father. None of them like to answer questions, especially those who have a lot of dirt to hide.

"Haven't you ever cared to know?" I ask.

Again, he flexes his jaw and then leans so close to me our noses nearly touch. "Don't ever worry about Arthur, I can handle him, and I'll it by any means necessary."

My stomach muscles clench as shivers run down my spine. "You sound like you're threatening violence."

He hasn't backed away. Our faces are still close and our breaths keep clashing.

"Holly, in your world there's peace and justice and following the rules. But men like Valentine don't respect your way of doing things," he whispers thickly, hotly, lustfully.

I'm moving more forward without thought. Our lips are closer. "If you think I live with pink clouds, unicorns, and fairies, you're wrong, Mr. Blackstone."

Jasper's mouth strikes like lightning, and his soft, warm tongue swirls indulgently around mine. My head spins. I'm dizzied by this hot passionate kiss of ours. He grips me by my waist, and together we stand, our bodies melting into each other. And this greedy way that we're kissing, palming each other, squeezing each other, all of a sudden takes a tender turn.

Our tongues brush, lips enmesh, my head floats as I bite back words I should not be saying to him at this juncture of our relationship. Jasper's large hands clamp down on my waist and he slowly walks me to the bed. My feet feel as if they're shuffling across air. It's Jasper and me, alone in the world. He lays me across the bed and takes off my shoes and spandex. Then he gently pulls me up into a sitting position, lifts my sweatshirt over my head. Our eyes remain locked on each other as he unhooks my bra-hook that's between my breasts and then removes my bra. He sucks air sharply between his teeth at the sight of my freed breasts. I understand that he's in control. I love it when Jasper is in the driver's seat. I love giving myself over to him. His warm and delicate mouth consumes one of my nipples, and his fingers crawl behind the crotch of my panties to penetrate my wetness. Arching my back, I tilt my head back and sigh from experiencing the overwhelming pleasure of his stimulation.

A spontaneous moan escapes him. "Oh Holly," he breathes, stepping away from me to take off his clothes as if we're in a race. "Get your panties off."

He doesn't have to say it twice, or frankly at all. I snatch my panties off and toss them.

Now that I'm naked and he's naked, Jasper takes me by the knees and parts them and then moves into me.

We are kissing again, and each of his thrusts feel so damn divine. But something is different about the way we're making love this time. We can't look away from each other. With every pump into me, I feel as if my heart will burst with an emotion I have worked so hard to stave off during our sex sessions. Every now and then, he'll close his eyes to bear the sensations of pleasure pouring to his cock. Then he'll stop prodding me but kiss me delicately, waiting for the feeling to weaken. I feel like a china store, and he's the bull who's trying to be careful.

"I'm falling for you," he whispers after our lips separate.

Jasper doesn't wait until I respond. He starts shifting in and out of me, faster and faster. He grabs hold of the headboard as if he trying to bust through me. I grip him tighter by his tapered waist, angling my burgeoning orgasm toward the action.

"You first," he says tightly.

I concentrate on the lines of pleasure sparking

through my sex. It's coming. My eyes are closed. I'm so close.

Jasper doesn't decelerate. "Please, baby. Do it, baby," he keeps repeating. Waiting to hear me. I can hear him straining to not let loose.

Right there...

And then... "I'm coming." And when it happens, I whimper and cry out to anyone who can hear me experience my orgasm spreading through my body.

And then, "Oh," Jasper shouts, convulsing. "I..."

JASPER HOLDS ME CLOSE, IT FEELS AS IF OUR BODIES are glued together. Every now and then, he'll kiss his favorite parts of my back, including my hot spot, which sends flickers of delight through me. There's no way we can sleep. We're not done making love yet. I don't think we'll ever be done making love. But now we're in recovery and I'm just so happy to have his hard body against mine.

"I've been wondering, why did you decide to become a reporter?" he asks.

I'm shocked he asked me that question simply

because it's such a first date question and we're way beyond the first date.

I snuggle closer against him and he draws me nearer. "I don't know," I say dreamily. "Maybe because I like to discover what lives beneath the surface of everything and everyone."

"You're really good at what you do," he says.

I purse my lips, fighting the urge to say more, to divulge more of the pain I keep to myself. But I trust Jasper Blackstone. I truly trust him. So my mouth opens, and I say, "I also became a journalist because I felt like my parents hid so much. It wasn't the stuff they paraded right in front of my face that hurt the most, like the double-dealing and petty crimes. They had deep and dark secrets that made them who they were and, as a result, made life feel so unsafe for me." Tears burn the backs of my eyes.

Jasper remains quiet, but he holds me tighter and with this sort of desperation as if he refuses to let me go. "I don't know my father's original sin," he finally says. "One sin covers the previous sin. Then one layers over that one. Then there's another and a million others. There are so many of them that I can't grasp the original sin. But the people who know what that sin is are around, holding my family hostage, threatening us."

I close my eyes to absorb what he just said. Was that a warning? I'm not sure.

"I heard what Arthur Valentine said about Bryn," I whisper.

Jasper's silent for a few beats. "You know I don't like that you went roaming through the tunnels."

I sigh, acquiescing. "I know." However, I'm not going to apologize for it. "But why did you show me that part of your home?"

Jasper laughs softly. Oh goodness, the way his body feels against mine when he laughs, I can become addicted to that feeling.

"I wasn't thinking clearly," he says, nudging his half-ready cock against me.

I suck air. That makes my sex shudder.

"I don't want to hurt your family, Jasper," I say with a sigh.

"I know that, Holly."

"But I think I know why Bryn asked me here. She wants me to uncover that original sin you mentioned earlier. And I think that she thinks it has something to do with Amelia." I wait to feel his body tense against me, but it doesn't. Then I'm struck softly by illumination. "I'm surprised you haven't tried to uncover the secret yourself. You don't strike me as someone who allows mystery to control his destiny."

Jasper presses his new full-blown erection against my butt again, and then guides me onto my back. "I am controlling my destiny."

Then, I moan as he thrusts his manhood inside me.

THE WEE HOURS OF THE MORNING

"I didn't care much for Randolph either," Jasper admits.

A lot of time has passed since Jasper and I climaxed. I can't mark the minutes or hours because we weren't counting them. I feel complete with my face against the left side of Jasper's chest, listening to the soft drum of his heart.

"But you were taught to be dutiful," I say.

He blows a long breath. "Yes, I know this." His body shifts abruptly. "Listen, I don't want this to end between us. Why don't you stick around?"

I twist my mouth thoughtfully. I've come to loathe the Blackstone mansion. It feels dark and unsettling, even if the cook is fantastic. Thinking about Bart's food makes my stomach growl.

"I'm hungry," I announce, purposely changing the subject.

"So am I." Jasper's finger slides up and down my clit under the covers.

A spontaneous sigh escapes me. "For food," I say tightly.

At this point, there's no need to hide our relationship. Jasper calls the kitchen and tells them to bring food for two to my room.

"So what do you say?" he asks as we wait for dinner to arrive.

My eyebrows pull. "Say about what?"

"Spending more time with me?"

My gaze scans the room and I frown. "I don't like this house."

His eyebrows flash up as he says, "Me either. But we'll stay in LA for a while and then go somewhere else."

"Like where?" My eyes dance with excitement.

"Anywhere in the world you want to go, baby. Let's get lost."

That's when I see that he's mostly dreaming. Jasper has a big problem to deal with and his name is Arthur Valentine. But if he's dreaming, then I'll let him.

"Okay," I say, smiling as someone knocks on the door.

We remain under the covers as the servers set up our dinner near the two high-backed chairs. They leave us a chilled bottle of champagne and then exit the room without giving us any dubious looks. I can only imagine the talk about us that's taking place in the laundry and kitchen.

We remain naked as we sit in the chairs, eating. I've never been this comfortable in the nude with anybody, I'm famished and eating like it. I only slow my pace when I realize he's grinning at me with amusement.

"Oh my God, your chef, Bart, is so *Top Chef All-Stars* winner," I say, chewing on the crispy peppered prime rib.

"Then he'll travel with us," he says like a king who made a new decree on the spot.

I narrow an eye suspiciously.

He narrows an eye curiously. "Do you not take me seriously?"

I shrug. "Kind of," I admit.

"My invitation is real, Holly."

"What about your business?"

"I have employees. I only hire the best. Plus, it's time I take a vacation, a real one."

If he's trying to ease my doubts, then he has succeeded.

"Okay." I grin blissfully. "Let's do it then. I mean, I can put off getting to work for as long as I want."

Jasper's eyes are alight. "Yeah?"

My smile stretches further. "Yeah."

Now his eyes smolder. "Good. Now, you eat that, and I'll eat you."

No Escape

HOLLY HENDERSON

DECEMBER 25TH

After eating, we of course made love again, and could no longer fight sleep. I slowly begin to stir when something hard grinds against my ass.

I moan to let him know that I'm awake and I feel him.

"Good morning beautiful," Jasper croons, his morning tone sends sparks of affection through my heart.

We make love and then shower together. Then, he leaves me to go dress himself in fresh clothes. Jasper and I are supposed to meet downstairs for breakfast in the small den rather than at the large table since it will only be the two of us. His siblings have made good on their claims and have all left the manor. I can sense the same restlessness in Jasper this morning. He's ready to get the hell out of Dodge too. But duty calls and he has to be the responsible, eldest brother.

His to-do list is long, so I'll have to do something to entertain myself until he's ready to go. He has to meet with the servants about revising their duties. None of them know Randolph is dead yet. They believe he's in the hospital being made comfortable as he endures his final stages of life. I learned that usually Bryn, and sometimes Asher, lives in the mansion. Spencer spends most of his time in Providence near his company's headquarters. But now, the house will sit empty. There's no family to wait on. Half the kitchen staff will be flown to Jasper's residence in Bel Air to wait on us. A skeleton crew of maids will keep the manor dusted. The gardeners will continue to shovel the snow, trim the trees, and rake the leaves. Jasper mentioned selling the manor one day; there's no need for him or his siblings to own it. They all hate the place.

However, before we catch our private flight to Los Angeles, we plan to make love one more time. I haven't brought any overtly sexy clothes, but now I wish I had. I want to give him a special treat for our last time making love in the place where we first started. So I go into Bryn's bedroom and find a white silk slip dress and put it on. My curves and tits look so tantalizing in the garment that I wonder if Jasper will be able to resist eating me rather than Bart's breakfast.

I'm surprised William doesn't meet me at the end of the hallway to escort me to the den. Jasper must've already released most of his house staff for the holidays and beyond. When I make it to the first floor, I head in the direction of where we are supposed to meet for breakfast. I hear Jasper shouting but I can't make out what he's saying. I hear another man's gruffer voice too. My heart beats a mile a minute. Something isn't right. So I change directions to go see what in the world is happening.

The noise leads me to the main foyer. I gasp and slap a hand over my constricted heart when I see the stone-faced, balding, and, evil-eyed, Arthur Valentine in the flesh. A young woman who appears to be in her late twenties or early thirties stands beside him. She has dark hair, almond eyes, and skin that looks as soft and new as a baby's bottom.

Arthur snarls at me. "Is that the whore of the house? I need a fuck right now. Maybe I can have a piece of her—for old times' sake."

I rub at my chest over my heart, feeling like I should escape those lewd eyes which give me the chills.

"Leave now," Jasper growls. His posture is strong. He looks as if he's ready to fight.

Arthur's face turns colder and more twisted when he finishes closing the distance between him and Jasper. He points to me. "That's Holly Henderson standing behind you, anything could happen to Harper while he's locked up." He burns me with the most evil eyes. "You know Harper, don't you? Harper Henderson?"

My head feels light and my legs want to shiver, but I stand strong. I know how to deal with threat against my father but the fact that I'm looking at Arthur Valentine is proof that skipping off into the sunset with Jasper is a very bad idea.

"Randolph is dead, and you're marrying my daughter today," Arthur says. "Or else…"

The woman keeps her beautiful doe eyes cast downward. There's something about her I find off. She's too submissive to be the daughter of such a man. I feel like she's acting.

Jasper's back muscles flex. I think he knows what Valentine means by 'or else.' He's a bad guy, and Jasper loves his family.

Valentine says something about my having fifteen minutes to clear the premises and step back into my pretty little life. Something inside me turns dim as my feet turn away from the former mobster who has gained some political and economic influence over the years, and his cunning daughter.

"Holly," Jasper calls after me.

"Let her go," Arthur says. "You have Bryn to think about."

I can feel Jasper tense up at the mention of his sister's name as I escape that scene. The deeper into the manor I advance, the less of Jasper's presence I feel. He's not dumb. He knows what he has to do. I know what he has to do. But what if he chooses to do the wrong thing?

I move fast, packing my suitcase. I throw my coat on over Bryn's dress, knowing she's never coming back for it. *Wow.* First Valentine threatened to harm my father and then Bryn. He's desperate. He needs Jasper to follow-through on whatever plan he's made with Randolph. That makes Arthur more dangerous than I first believed him to be.

Soon, I'm tossing my luggage into the trunk of my car and driving off the property. I only catch a peripheral glance of a stretch limousine with tinted windows parked out front, sitting in the same spot where Jasper knocked on my window five days ago. *Gosh… five days ago.* It feels like I've been here for five months. Arthur is still at the house. His threats have worked. He has managed to keep Jasper from following his heart. The pain in my chest is too much to bear. Tears rush to my eyes, and I sob.

TWO WEEKS LATER

I sit at the desk in my small office downtown. The new year has come, and I'm still trying to immerse myself in work. It's the best way to forget about Jasper Blackstone. However, I can't concentrate much on any new assignment. I miss my holiday lover and regret we can't throw all of our responsibilities to the wind and travel like we had planned. I miss Jasper's touch. His delicious scent. I constantly crave him inside me. I thought I'd be over him sooner rather than later, but that is not the case.

And developments about the Blackstones have mounted. The day after Christmas, after returning to Philadelphia, I'd received a call from Kylie. She told me that the address Gina gave me in Chattanooga belongs to an old, abandoned and dilapidated house that was last officially owned by the Greer family.

"The Greers were poor as dirt and had six daughters. That's all I could figure out so far."

"Thanks," I said.

"Holly, that didn't sound enthusiastic at all."

I sighed tiredly. "Listen, I'm over the Blackstones. I really don't care about them anymore."

"Oh no," she sighed. "Which one were you screwing?"

Of course, I denied having sexual relations with any of them. I basically told Kylie that they were a weird family and I just didn't care anymore.

She remained silent for a while then said, "I see. Well, I'm going to let you cool off for a while and then get back to you. I'm unable to investigate the

Blackstones, but you are, and I want to get to the bottom of this."

I had agreed to talk with her about the family at a later date so that I could get her off the phone, go to bed, crawl under the sheets, and weep.

I'm surprised she hasn't gotten back to me as of yet. I haven't changed my mind though. I want nothing to do with the Blackstones. Then I stop scanning the AP newswire as my eyes remain stuck on the details of a story. Bryn Blackstone is considered a missing person. Her Mercedes was found along a California highway, keys still in the ignition, and her cell phone and wallet in the passenger seat. Authorities were led to question a man they considered to be her boyfriend, Dale Rumor, a clerk who worked for Judge Robert Kristoff, but he also cannot be found. Blood was found in Bryn's car, hers on the steering wheel and Dale's in the back seat. Crime scene investigators believe foul play is probable.

I cough because I had forgotten to breathe. "No…" *Please no.*

Bryn and Dale murdered? My mind quickly puts the pieces together. I spring to my feet, feeling as if I have to do something. Then there's a gentle knock on my office door. I press my hand over my heart, hoping it's a miracle. I was thinking of Bryn, therefore I hope it's her.

"Come in," I call impatiently.

The door opens, and the shock of who it is makes me lean back so far that I almost lose my balance. "What are you doing here?"

The journey continues in *Desire,* book two.

The Blackstone Brothers Series

Jasper's Story
Intrigued (Book 1)
Desire (Book 2)
Claimed (Book 3)

———

Spencer's Story
Enthrall (Book 1)
Impulse (Book 2)
Bliss (Book 3)
Bonus Book!
Exposed (Spencer & Jada Bonus Book)

Asher's Story

Seduction (Book 1)

Embrace (Book 2)

Bryn's Story

Destined

About the Author

Z.L. has been writing romance full-time since 2011, which has allowed her to amass quite a catalog of romance novels. She loves what she does, and as she's evolved, so have her stories. Now, she's focused on writing brooding and loyal, billionaire heroes, and the smart, plucky heroines they can't live without.

When Z.L.'s not writing, she loves to cook and read good books, which have the power to take her somewhere she's never been.

For more information:
zlarkadiebooks.com
contact@zlarkadiebooks.com

Printed in Great Britain
by Amazon

35977964R00155